W9-CEU-738

YF
OUG   Oughton, Jerrie.
             Music from a
           place called Half
           Moon

98

HAYNER PUBLIC LIBRARY DISTRICT
ALTON, ILLINOIS

OVERDUES .10 PER DAY. MAXIMUM FINE
COST OF BOOKS. LOST OR DAMAGED BOOKS
ADDITIONAL $5.00 SERVICE CHARGE.

DEMCO

Music from a
Place Called Half Moon

Music from a Place Called Half Moon

Jerrie Oughton

Houghton Mifflin Company
Boston 1995

HAYNER PUBLIC LIBRARY DISTRICT
ALTON, ILLINOIS

Turn Your Eyes Upon Jesus by Helen H. Lemmel copyright © 1922 by Singspiration Music/ASCAP. All rights reserved. Used by permission of Benson Music Group, Inc.

Copyright © 1995 by Jerrie Oughton

All rights reserved. For information about permission to reproduce selections from this book, write to Permissions, Houghton Mifflin Company, 215 Park Avenue South, New York, New York 10003.

Library of Congress Cataloging-in-Publication Data

Oughton, Jerrie.
    Music from a place called Half Moon / by Jerrie Oughton.
    p. cm.
    Summary: In 1956 in Half Moon, North Carolina, thirteen-year-old Edie Jo comes to terms with her own prejudice and the death of a friend.
    ISBN 0-395-70737-4
    [1. Prejudices — Fiction. 2. Friendship — Fiction. 3. Indians of North America — Fiction. 4. Race relations — Fiction. 5. Death — Fiction. 6. Family life — Fiction.] I. Title.
PZ7.0897Mu 1995   94-25368
[Fic] — dc20   CIP
                AC

Printed in the United States of America

BP 10 9 8 7 6 5 4 3 2 1

With much gratitude I would like to acknowledge the enthusiastic support and help that was given to me by the following people: extended family member, Randal Ewing; our daughter, Cher Oden and her son, Kyle; the members of my writing group, Writers, Ink; my long-time friend and inspiration, Dr. Martha Gurwitt; my husband and dearest friend, Paul; and Margaret Raymo, my wonderfully wise editor.

For my Jonah

Music from a
Place Called Half Moon

1

My brother, Jonah, taught me to be afraid of the dark. Funny how Jonah's word was gospel to me. In a way, he was my hero. I believed just about anything he'd tell me. And Jonah had taught me careful, like it was his job. He was just being plumb ornery, but I didn't know that then.

First, it had been the dark inside our house. He had begun early. I had been three or four when he'd say, "Look-a-there, Hot Shot. See those eyes peering out from the closet? He's waiting till the house gets dark. Then he's gonna come out mean and growling."

Of course Mama and Daddy were never around. It was like Jonah carried the fears in his hip pocket, hidden till he wanted to pull them out.

Next it was the dark outside. I must have been six then but still believed . . . believed in the tooth fairy and Santa Claus and all that a big brother could conjure up and paint in my mind.

"Right over there behind them bushes. See it creeping, stealthy?"

And finally it was just night itself I was afraid of.

And anything related to darkness.

I remember thinking that spring of 1956 when I was thirteen, *Surely to goodness a person outgrows her fears.* But that spring I learned yet another.

That was the wettest spring that folks in these parts ever recollected. Flash floods. Drenching, creek-choking rains. Our town of Half Moon, North Carolina, lay twenty-two miles due south of Asheville. Its seven thousand six hundred and thirty-two residents were tucked on the sides of three mountains, deep in the rain-drenched Smokies. Of that number, three hundred and seventeen were Indians and half-breeds, and two families were black.

Come early April, when the French Broad River was on the rise, two Indians were drowned. That left three hundred and fifteen, not that anybody much noticed. I surely didn't know them. The only reason I took notice was that it gave me one more thing to be afraid of. Death. I read the account in the *Half Moon Weekly* and pictured in my mind what it would be like under the dark, rushing water. That's when I added another fear to my collection, like a person would add charms to a bracelet.

I wrote about this in a book I had got for my thirteenth birthday. It was an empty book to fill with my thoughts. All fall and winter I had written poems and fragments of my mind. But more and more my thoughts all ground down to that one thing. Fear.

Even at school, it formed an undercurrent for the way I was. And there I learned a different kind of fear.

The eighth graders were stuck in the gymnasium every day for health and phys. ed. Neither one was my favorite but I could abide them. It was Fridays, square-dancing days, that I dreaded. They stirred fires in my insides that began sometime after supper on Thursday evenings and licked away even while I slept. I wasn't up to dancing with a boy yet, even if it was just square dancing. I hoped to God I'd be sick every Friday that dawned.

"Stand next to me, Edie Jo," my best friend, Mary Grady Heldron, hissed in my ear a Friday morning in April of that year.

"Quit spitting on me," I told her. "I ain't budging. I ain't dancing."

"All right! All you girls make an inner circle and you boys form a circle outside the girls." That was Miss Biggers, a wide woman with arms that were flabbier than Jell-O. Those exercises weren't doing her any good. Square dancing was her hobby, so Fridays she perked up like a revived dandelion. "Circle up!" she shouted.

Naturally the boys made their circle facing out so all we could see of them was their ducktail haircuts and the backs of their low-slung pants.

"All right, fellas, face those girls. Boys, slide to the right in time to the music. Girls, the same! Stop when the music stops."

Miss Biggers shouted all this at an ear-splitting screech, voice tighter than a pumped-up basketball.

When we went to the right for the second time, I

wound up with one of the three Indian boys in class for a partner. Cherokee Fish. A half-breed. Nobody knew his real name. At least not us. Everybody had always called him Cherokee. The other two Indian boys wouldn't have anything to do with him, didn't even live near him, since he was only half Indian. The white boys hated him because he was only half white. Me? I hated him because he was a boy. He had failed two grades. Maybe even three. I knew that his little sister, Leona, was catching up to him fast in school. But the look on that boy's face said he hadn't missed anything. Said he'd done things most of us eighth graders hadn't even heard about. The half smile on his face was his natural look. I'd never seen him without it.

We danced together but he never even bothered to look at me, which suited me just fine.

"Now we're gonna try something different," Miss Biggers said after we'd square-danced awhile. "I can't let you people out of eighth grade without learning how to slow-dance."

Everybody groaned. This was going to be worse even than square dancing.

"Watch me while I show you how to do the box step."

She grabbed at Skeeter Runyon to use him as her partner in her demonstration, but he shot under her arm and sprinted into a wall of guys who hooted loud.

"All right then. You," she said, pointing to Cherokee Fish. "You come here, Mr. Fish."

He pointed to himself and mouthed, "Me?"

"Yes, you," she said. "Come here."

He swaggered over and stood beside her, facing us all, his half smile smack in place.

"Face me," she told him.

He did.

"Hoo-hoo-hooo, Cherokee. You gon' do a war dance for us?" Skeeter Runyon called out, and his voice bounced all around that gymnasium.

Cherokee shook his head real slow-like and called over his shoulder to Skeeter. "Nope. Thought I'd try a rain dance since we ain't seen rain in so long."

The boys all howled.

Miss Biggers stepped toward them to quieten them down. That was when Cherokee Fish reached over behind his shoulder and tugged out a make-believe arrow from a make-believe quiver strapped to his back. He fitted it into a bow that wasn't there either, took aim right at Miss Biggers's large rear end, and let fly. Then he laid the make-believe bow on the floor.

Everybody busted out laughing and hollering.

I haven't ever seen a teacher have that hard a time quietening people down in my life. She hadn't the first notion what had caused us all to go to pieces like that. She climbed up on the bleachers and hollered and hollered.

Finally, she yelled out, "Sit down right where you're at!"

We buckled under and got ourselves good and gritty on the wood gym floor. All except Skeeter.

"Take a seat, Mr. Runyon!" she screamed. It wasn't

hard to tell she was walking close to the edge of a prec-
ipice.

"I already got one," he called back, grinning and
lounging his elbow on the caged-window sill.

Miss Biggers's face got plumb red. She opened up her
wide mouth and flew at Skeeter like a hen pecking up
a bug in dirt.

"Then put it on the damn floor!" she screeched.

You've never heard a bunch of people get quiet so
fast in your life. Teachers didn't all the time cuss. Especially not women teachers. Skeeter turned white and
slithered on down to the floor.

And that was the calmest part of the afternoon. After
Miss Biggers showed Cherokee Fish how to do the box
step, and she made us all pair up, boy-girl, and do it,
too, then she made another mistake. She paired up Cherokee with Darnella Hendrix, who had been going steady
with Skeeter Runyon since fifth grade. There wasn't
anything wrong with that, at first. They box-danced
around like us all until a boy made like to shoot an
arrow at Darnella, after he called out to Cherokee to
snag his attention.

Cherokee reached round to Darnella's backside,
where the arrow would have lit, and he yanked it out
for her, which would have been the polite thing to do,
had it been a real arrow. Skeeter didn't take kindly to
it, though, being as she was his girl. He lunged at Cherokee like he was gonna knock his head off.

"Hey, man." Cherokee broke Skeeter's hold with his

arm before it ever got lodged good. "Cool your jets. That was in fun. I didn't even touch her. Okay?"

"Okay?" Skeeter growled and his jaw jutted out a mile while he glared at Cherokee. "No, you son-of-a-bitchin' half-breed. You touch my woman again and I'll tear off your head. You'll be the first headless Cherokee in Half Moo —"

The swiftness in Cherokee Fish's move made blurs out of his arms. He grabbed Skeeter Runyon's shirt collar and, twisting it, pulled his face so close to his own that they were breathing for each other.

"Don't never call me a half-breed again," Cherokee whispered to Skeeter's nostrils. There wasn't any smile on Cherokee's face at that point. He was serious as sin. "You got that straight?"

Skeeter's face was beginning to be deep red and his eyes were sort of bugging out, but he didn't make an answer.

Cherokee gave him a jerk, his hand twisting harder on Skeeter's shirt collar. That oxford-cloth shirt wasn't giving an eighth of an inch on Skeeter's windpipe.

"Yes," he finally whispered.

Cherokee's lips sucked together tight and he looked hard and long into someplace inside Skeeter's bulging eyes. Then he let him go. Not a shove backwards or anything. Just undid his hand to his shirt collar. Then that boy turned and left. Left Skeeter Runyon crooked forward, gasping at any and all air. Left us all standing, bunched under the ten-foot hoop with the torn net. It wasn't basketball season, so they hadn't fixed it yet. It wasn't the right time for Skeeter Runyon either, it appeared to me.

And that's when I strung that third fear onto my collection. I wasn't exactly sure what all I was afraid of yet. People who were different — different color, different way of living, and mad because they knew they were different and didn't know how to live with it, how to use it — they scared me. I had seen it in Cherokee Fish's face before he left. His eyes said that without a doubt he felt he was different, less somehow . . . somehow lacking. And he hated it.

2

That next week in April held more than any of us ever bargained for. On Saturday the fifteenth, something happened that would change our lives forever. The phone had rung about seven o'clock in the evening and Mr. George Findley screamed in my daddy's ear that Gramma's house was burning.

We tore fast down the mountain to town, hearing the fire sirens as we flew. As we rounded the corner, I could see that the whole block was lit from my gramma's house. It was a torch against the night. It was the hottest fire I had ever seen. I had never watched a house burn before. And the smell! It was a bitter, scorching smell that made people squint. I watched the faces in the light of the fire. But if I'd been a blind person, I would have still known the fire by the sounds and the feel. Heavy hoses slapped the pavement, and water gushed; you could hear little explosions and falling lumber and people shouting. You could feel the heat from across the street in the Findleys' yard where we stood.

Me and Mama and Gramma went to our house after

we knew there was no hope. That was when I called Mary Grady Heldron.

She was the person I called on Christmas morning to tell what presents I got; I was the phone call she made on her birthday to say what all she got; and she was the person I called that April night my gramma came to be with us. The night my gramma's house caught fire and burned to the ground.

"Caught fire?"

"That's what I said."

"Burned down?"

"I just told you, Mary Grady." Lord, she was slow to grasp it.

"Edie Jo Houp, you're telling a big one. To the ground?"

"That's what I said."

"How'd it get started?"

"Nobody knows. The fireman got my gramma out and the living-room sofa. That was it. The fire got so hot they couldn't go back in," I told her.

The morning after, Mrs. Heldron brought over an apple cake and she and Mary Grady rode with us to see where my gramma's house had stood.

"Looks like a giant cricket," Mary Grady said, "with his skinny back legs forking up in the air."

It did look like a cricket, the second floor beams all burned black and still hot and smoking, standing broken over.

"Reckon when your gramma'll build it back?" Mary Grady asked, puffing at her hair. It was longer than mine and curled, but always seemed like it fell across her face and she was forever blowing it away.

"Never," I told her, walking along the sidewalk toward the Ninth Street corner so Mama couldn't hear me. She and Gramma were standing on the front-yard grass with Mrs. Heldron. Talking. "There wasn't no insurance money to speak of, Daddy said," I told Mary Grady. "What Gramma's got saved up'll go for Jayhue Smith's wrecking crew to come in and demolish it."

"Demolish it?"

"Mary Grady, why do you say everything after me?" I asked her.

She flounced over to where her mama stood and planted those skinny legs facing west. I didn't care. Talking with an echo was the last thing I had in mind that morning.

Gramma moved into my room and I was set up in the living room, with a feather mattress on a cot for a bed and Mama's folding silk screen for a privacy wall. There wasn't even a chest of drawers or bureau, so I took Gerber baby-food boxes cut low so they'd slide under the cot, and that's where I kept my underwear and socks. My dresses hung from two big cup hooks Daddy had sunk in the wood frame on either side of one of the two huge living-room windows. Too tall and wide for window shades. On the wall Daddy had hung a mirror. Some mirrors gloss right over a person's faults. This one magnified them, made my dark hair straighter, my face whiter.

"This here's right nice," my brother, Jonah, felt compelled to say after I got it all set up.

I just looked at him. Seventeen years of living hadn't given him a brain yet.

"Right nice?" I asked.

He looked at me with those cold eyes.

"Right nice would be having walls," I told him. "And a bulletin board and a closet and a bookcase. But, maybe it won't be forever."

"Don't trust your luck."

"What d'you mean by that?"

He stretched out on the cot and hung a foot and a half beyond. I could see now why Mama hadn't stuck him out here.

"Hot Shot, I don't think Gramma'll ever move back. She'll be right here in this house the day I leave home to go to college and the day you leave home . . ."

"To go to college," I finished for him.

"Right." But I could tell he didn't think that would ever happen.

"Now, Hot Shot, I wouldn't worry about anybody looking in these windows." He ambled over to the front window and looked out it. "They'd have to get up on the porch to look in this one at the foot of the bed, and the window at the side of the house, there, it's pretty high up. They'd have to be a tall mother to see in that window. I wouldn't worry about it none, Hot Shot."

"I'm not," I snapped because from that minute on, when dark filled the window glass, I'd remember what he said, feeling eyes on me, following me, watching me sleep. I might not have even thought about the dark outside if he hadn't brought it up. But now that he had, it was all I'd hold in my head every time night fell and found me in that corner.

So I found a way around it. I slept with all the lights off so nobody would be able to look in the windows and watch me. No more night light for me. For once, the dark inside was more of a comfort than a fear, a hiding place from the world out the windows. It was the way I learned to live, behind the silk screen, out of boxes, in the dark.

Staring out those windows into the darkness, I couldn't tell if what I saw was real or just my mind's doing. And sometimes I missed seeing things that were right there in front of me all along.

It was that last part, missing seeing the important things that were there all along . . . I learned to look differently that summer I was thirteen, and things were never the same again.

Monday evening Sheriff Stringfield showed up at our front door, talking to Daddy about arson. I had lived to be thirteen years of age and had never even heard the word, but I learned fast. Those two sat out in the front-porch swing to do their talking, and I just rested on the foot of my cot by the open window so I could catch on to arson.

"Horace, rack your brain now. Tell me, can you think of a soul who'd be holding a grudge against your mother?"

I watched Daddy shake his head, slow and wondering. "Not a soul."

The sheriff stretched and brushed dirt from his trouser leg with big, fat slaps. "Well," he said in between slaps, "our boys have conclusive evidence this thing was started on purpose." He stopped slapping and looked over at Daddy. "Unfortunately, the arsonist didn't leave much of a calling card. Or, leastwise, not one we can read yet. They always leave a calling card."

"A definitive clue?" Daddy asked.

Sheriff Stringfield nodded.

"What did you find so far?" Daddy asked him.

"Well . . ." Then the sheriff dropped his voice low and laid it out for Daddy, too soft for me to catch all he said. I heard words now and then, *bundle* and *kerosene,* and long stretches of low talk that I couldn't make out. Once in a while a word popped out, just making it worse. I had been figuring that Gramma's little teakettle of cinnamon on the stove had burned itself dry and caught the house on fire. That had been my private theory. But what caused the fire hadn't been near as vital to me as the results of the fire. Now, come to find out, that fire came from kerosene and a bundle.

"So . . ." The sheriff stood and stretched. I shifted

sideways against the wall, lest he turn my way. ". . . see what you can find out, Horace. Ask her if she has any enemies or had a run-in with somebody."

Daddy got up out of the swing. I could hear the chains moving.

"I'll talk to her," he said.

"And remember," Sheriff Stringfield said, "this is in confidence. We want everybody to keep right on thinking the fire was an accident. It's harder to catch an arsonist if he thinks we've found a calling card."

3

It was the very next Wednesday when I got off the school bus that I saw my gramma for the first time. Really saw her. She was one of those things in the dark of my mind I hadn't counted on, and I bumped flat into her before I saw her.

Actually I heard her long before I saw her. When I hopped off the bus and ran down the drive, I thought the house was empty because the car was gone. But when I stepped up on the front porch, I heard a sound like wind makes on house corners as it tears itself making the turn. It was a wailing sound. Mournful. When I opened the front door, it was louder. Then it stopped. But I followed to where I had heard it.

"Gramma," I called. "That you?"

I heard her blowing into a handkerchief. She always carried one tucked in her belt on the left. So she could snatch it with her right hand when she needed it.

When I rounded the door frame of my old room, I spied her, there in my rocking chair. She had her handkerchief held to her mouth, mashing it tight.

"Gramma?" I whispered it because the quiet was so

solid I didn't want to wrinkle it and scare her. "Gramma?"

She looked up at me over her pressed handkerchief, and her eyes behind her round glasses brimmed over.

I dragged the dresser stool up beside her and held on to her shoulders that were shaking with her crying. Now and again she'd take a deep breath and then go at it once more. I knew she had cause to be hurting, but I had lost out, too. And I hadn't shed a tear for my loss. I'd lost my room and I didn't even have drawers for socks anymore. So I just sat and patted her shoulder.

After about a quarter of an hour she pulled herself together and spoke up.

"Edie. Edie Jo," she said real croaky. She cleared up her throat but her voice kept sounding like a rusty hinge on the edge of quitting. "Every last thing I ever had is gone."

I thought about Gramma's house, about the long hall through the middle of it where you could see, when you stood at her front door, clean through to the back yard.

"My scrapbooks and photo albums," she whispered, like they were dead people. "Pictures of when your daddy was a boy. His drawing he brought home from school on the first day he was in first grade. I recollect it exactly. 'Twas a picture of children on a playground, some standing on their heads."

I remembered seeing that picture in a scrapbook. I used to perch on Gramma's bed and thumb through her albums while she sewed at her sewing machine, wearing her green eyeshade and listening to her radio programs. I began to miss her house, too.

"All my crocheting," she said. "All gone up in smoke."

I remembered her crocheting. Her doilies and bedspreads and snowflakes she'd crocheted that hung all in her Christmas tree every year. I remembered the smell in Gramma's house. It smelled like Christmas all year. Sort of cinnamon and ginger from the little brass teakettle she kept simmering on an eye of her stove. And the living room all shiny with sunlight bouncing off photographs in frames all over the room. I was in there four times, three on the wall and one on a table. And Jonah. And Mama and Daddy on their wedding day. Somebody had tinted that picture and made Mama's hair redder than it was. Either that or her hair had turned browner in twenty years.

"Edie Jo," Gramma said from the place where she was, "I don't know I'll ever be at peace again. I feel like an actual part of me has burned up."

The spaces in between her talking got shorter. "I have lost every Irving Berlin recording I ever owned," she said, looking at me like I would know what that meant.

"Who's he?" I asked her.

"Irving Berlin is the greatest songwriter ever born. He wrote most songs you hear. He wrote "White Christmas." Not a minute passes that one of his songs isn't being played on a radio somewhere. I used to pop a record in the Victrola and listen to his music when I went about my housework."

She rocked and sat and watched the wallpaper by the bed with eyes deader than the eyes in my Shirley Temple doll still sitting on my bookcase in the corner.

"He wrote me a letter once," she said. "I wrote him first and he wrote me back."

"Who?"

"Irving Berlin. The letter burned up, too."

Seemed to me Gramma had been collecting up these memories for four days. She hadn't cried since after that first night. And now, suddenly, the cork had exploded out of a bottle in her mind, and whatever was inside came out in a rush. There wasn't any comforting her, either. Before Mama drove up from grocery shopping at the Piggly Wiggly, I had begun to join Gramma in that place where she had gone to. That place made Gerber baby-food boxes for socks and underwear seem unimportant, made those boxes seem like the best bureau drawers a person ever had.

Gramma and I heard Mama's car rolling in on the gravel in the driveway at the same time.

"Law me," Gramma said, hurrying to stand up. "I don't want to seem ungrateful."

She took off down the hall to the bathroom and I went for the front door to help Mama with her sacks of groceries.

My mama would have been a pretty woman if she

had covered up her freckles with makeup. Mine were coming on and I planned to plaster makeup across them till they were hid. But my mama's hair made you almost overlook the freckles anyway. It was her crowning glory. It curled right on its own and bounced when she walked. She kept it bobbed short to her neck. I'd have given an arm and a leg if I could have had curly hair like Mama's. Jonah got it, though, and I got daddy's hair, straight, hair so silky that it worked its way out of a braid inside of ten minutes.

I watched Mama's hair bounce as I followed her down our long hallway into the dining room we never used and on into the kitchen.

I don't guess Mama ever knew that Gramma had gone on a crying jag because, by the time me and Mama had put up groceries and cooked up supper, Gramma strolled in the kitchen like she'd just finished listening to her afternoon soap operas and was going to set the table next. I did notice that the powder she had dabbed on her nose covered up all the redness.

"What're you working on?" she asked Mama. It amazed me how a person could be so low they were sobbing, and twenty-five minutes later they looked fresher than a daisy.

"Prune whip," Mama said, laying the bowl to one side.

It was Mama's favorite dessert, next to pineapple upside-down cake. If I had to choose between the two, I guess a forced choice would be pineapple upside-down cake. But neither one of them could touch desserts like homemade ice cream or cherry pie with lattice crust on the top or ten-egg pound cake. Prune whip was too full of air for me. And just knowing that something as nasty as a prune went into it curled my hair.

Jonah and I had this one thing in common, our hatred of prunes. And, wouldn't you know — we had to be born into a family where the mama believed in prunes like they were kin to God. Mama was all the time asking us, "Did you eat your prune yet today?" It didn't matter morning, noon, or night. Just so you ate one.

"Why would I want to?" I had asked her one time.

"Because," she had said, then whispered, "it keeps you reg'lar."

I went on that for the next few years, eating one prune a day, and then one day I thought to ask her, "Mama, what does *reg'lar* mean?"

"What?" she had asked.

"Reg'lar. You know," I said, making sure she wasn't misunderstanding me because I was too soft. "Reg'lar. The reason you eat a prune every day."

My question was a good one. It was just that my timing was off. We'd been sitting in church waiting for Sunday evening vespers service to commence. It made Mama so hopping mad that I'd asked the question there, and asked it loud enough for people in the choir loft to hear, that she turned redder than a traffic light on stop. Daddy explained it to me on the way back home, that *reg'lar* had to do with going to the bathroom.

Well, that church experience was a pure tea party compared to what took place that Wednesday night at church, the night Mama served prune whip for dessert. I wondered if the prune whip was an ill omen, things being ragged from that supper on. Mama washed, and I dried and nearly dropped two glasses.

"Edie Jo," Mama snapped, "you be careful with them tumblers."

"Ain't nothin' but jelly jars," I said under my breath.

"Don't you be sassing me, young lady," she said, and her voice was sharper than the knives I had started drying on. I guessed getting used to one extra person in the house was wearing on her nerves.

On the way to Wednesday night prayer meeting, Gramma sat between Jonah and me in the back seat of the car. She was wearing a shawl, but where it didn't cover I could feel her warm, smooth skin touching me and it was a comfort. In church, I sat right up next to her to stay warm. April evenings take on a chill in the mountains, and the church furnace hadn't worked since the floods in March and early April.

The service itself went along all right. We sang my favorite song, "Turn Your Eyes upon Jesus." Gramma's voice wandered around the notes, never hitting them dead on, but there wasn't any way you could mess up that hymn.

If we had only left after the church service like about a third of the people did, everything would have been all right. But, since Daddy was a deacon, he always

stayed for the church business meeting. They were discussing whether or not to have an *open* Vacation Bible
School that summer.

Mr. John Guthrie, over to the back right, stood and
said he believed we ought to take care of our own children and not try to nurture the whole town of Half
Moon.

That was when my daddy shot up from his seat like
Mama had dug a fingernail in him. He's a tall man,
anyway. Tall and skinny. And when he stands, he towers
over top of people. Even when they're standing. But we
were sitting, and he looked like the giant David cut
down with the slingshot, he was so tall.

"I believe," he started off real slow in his voice that's
so low it shuts out daylight, "I believe that the mission
of a church is to nurture a whole community, John." I
guessed he was talking to Mr. Guthrie, who had sat
back down. "If we take care of our own children, that
is merely self-serving."

His voice wasn't unkind. Just firm.

"Well then, what?" a woman said from three pews
behind us. "What do you propose? If you open Vacation
Bible School to every child in Half Moon, Horace Houp,
you'll have more half-breeds than you will whites. I
wouldn't object to one or two, but not hordes of them,
don't you know."

The "don't you know" clued me in to who it was. I
didn't even have to turn around to see it was old Mrs.
Hensinger. What did she care anyway who came to

Vacation Bible School? Even her grandchildren were too old to come. The tension in her voice sounded like she had heavy stakes in it, though. Like she was going to have to brush shoulders with half-breeds and the results were going to be fatal at the very least.

Daddy turned all the way round to get her in his sights before he answered her. And then he didn't answer in a hurry. He took his time thinking through words until he came to just the right ones.

"Madam," he began tender, and I knew he was gonna zing her good, "Madam, if only *one* white child attends Vacation Bible School and the rest are Indians, this church will be fulfilling its God-given duty because the Great Commission says, 'Go into all the world and preach the gospel.' That's *all* the world, not just to lily-white children. *All* the world. Not just Vine Street Baptist Church. *All* the world." If nothing else, my daddy knew how to hammer a point home.

And what made me really mad was that I wasn't sure if he was in this discussion because in his heart he believed God meant us to hold Vacation Bible School for people of all colors or because he just loved a good fight. Either one could have been possible. I had never seen him out palling around with anybody of color.

Nobody in the whole church spoke for a spell, and then suddenly people were talking from all four corners and in the middle, too. At one time. Over top of each other. From the third pew from the front, we were in a position to see and hear it all, and I never heard such a free-for-all in my born days. Nobody was listening to what anybody else was saying. It reminded me of what we read in class about Chinese schools, everybody doing their lessons out loud. Every once in a while I'd hear a "don't you know" and know for a fact Mrs. Hensinger was still in it hot and heavy.

Right when I was thinking we'd probably be in the same shape the next morning when the sun came up, my gramma stood up and did the strangest thing I've ever seen her do. Or anybody do. And, if it hadn't worked, she'd have been mighty embarrassed. Not nearly as embarrassed as me, but embarrassed.

She sidled out of her end of the pew, past Jonah. I figured she was making a trip to the ladies' room, but no. She turned toward the front of the church. I figured she was just confused and as soon as she got her bearings, she'd veer left on out the door down to the front. But no. She knew right where she was heading. She climbed the stairs to the pulpit. Walked straight to the rack where the Bible sits and the preacher preaches from. With the microphone. Then she leaned in toward the mike.

So far, maybe four people in the church even knew she was there. Three of them were in our pew. Daddy was still facing the back and hadn't seen her yet. I wondered what in sweet Jesus' name she was going to say. I didn't know but what me and Mama and Jonah might want to be heading out the back door lest she get all these angry people to unite and be mad at her. They were mad enough at Daddy already.

But she didn't say one word. She opened her mouth and started singing. Right soft and quaky at first. But when she got under way, she evened on out and for the most part hit close to the notes.

Turn your eyes upon Jesus,
Look full in His wonderful face.
And the things of earth will grow strangely dim
In the light of His glory and grace.

She didn't stop there, either. Not even slow down. She dug right into the next part. Her voice sort of whispered and warbled over the loudspeaker system, and people started winding down and turning to see who was singing in the middle of the biggest fight the Vine Street Baptist Church had had in years.

Daddy was the first to join her. He started right in the middle of the second verse with her. Mama stood up alongside Daddy then and sang, too. Before I stood, I saw her slip her hand inside his.

If the singing had healed the differences, that would have been the other half of the miracle, the first half being that the entire church sang that hymn all the way outside and never said another cross word. Till they reached home. But plenty must have been said then.

I thought April evenings were chilly, but they weren't anything compared to days when your daddy wants to integrate a town that's digging its hind feet into the dirt the whole nine yards. There wasn't any way on this earth the white people in Half Moon were going to be integrated with half-breeds — or full-blooded Indians, for that matter.

I heard it at every corner, too.

"My cousin Elbert came over to our house last night," this girl named Frankie Everson told me before school on Thursday when I was digging in my locker for a pencil.

I found the pencil and turned and looked at her. "So? What?"

She made sure to have my full attention and then said, "He wanted to tell my mama how your daddy loves half-breeds."

I just stared at her.

"Do you love half-breeds like your daddy does?"

I've never wanted to slap anybody so bad in my life. What I couldn't figure, though, was whether I was madder at my daddy or Frankie Everson.

4

The chill around Half Moon because of my daddy's outspokenness got so bad I started in taking evening walks just to get away, to be right by myself with my thoughts. I thought about integration and what it meant on a daily basis. I wasn't sure part of me wasn't with old Mrs. Hensinger. I could take an Indian or two at one time. I even danced with Cherokee Fish, when I was forced to. But having them to your house? Drinking out of your glasses and sitting at your table? I was pretty sure I wasn't ready for that. Might never be.

Sometimes I thought about arson and how it had already eaten into my life. That was easier to think about than integration. Arson had happened. There was no controlling that. Integration was still ahead and might need some limits set on it.

Dark was longer and longer coming in May, but I made sure I was home before night fell. I surely did not want to be out roaming when night hit because, in the mountains, there's no such thing as twilight. It goes from daylight to dark in one breath. So I made sure to turn back before the light was gone.

One evening I hiked myself to the sawmill halfway up a little mountain near our house. I had found it the summer I was seven. It was just far enough away to be somewhere else without taking hours to get there. There was a logging road that led up there for trucks, but I took a path I knew, threading through thick woods. It was more direct. This time of day the sawmill men had already left. I passed on through the empty clearing, past the buildings and the sawdust pile, and took big stones crossing the creek. The same one that ran on down to my house. There was a rocky ledge that overlooked the side of the mountain. I sat down there and leaned against a pine tree and watched cars on the highway down below.

I reckon I'd been sitting for about ten minutes when I heard a noise like an animal breaking through bushes and dried leaves. I looked over across the creek to where the noise was coming from and I began to see something black in the shadows, moving fast toward the clearing. Every muscle in my body tensed up, thinking it might be a bear. What else could be that black?

But when it reached the clearing and left the trees, I saw it wasn't a bear after all. It was worse. It was that Cherokee Fish boy in a black T-shirt.

What in God's name is he doing here? I thought, beginning to panic. I had seen what he did to Skeeter Runyon. My whole body let go itself and all my fear was centered right in my chest while the rest of me went limp. If I'd been standing, I'd have fallen down.

He looked around, spied a sawhorse the sawmill men use, and moved over to it. Hiking up his pants, he lifted himself up backwards onto it. Then he shot right back down to the ground. He reached in his pocket, dug down deep, and pulled out something that flashed silver in the late afternoon sun.

Oh, God! A gun, I thought, and my mouth dropped down to let in more air to my chest. There wasn't any way I could ever get enough air. There wasn't any way I could escape, either, especially if he had a gun.

Settle down, Edie Jo Houp, I said to myself. *What's the worst thing that's going to be possible?*

When I answered that question, I was even more afraid. Either he could target-practice and hit me by accident. Then, seeing what he'd done, he'd just finish me off right there. Roll my body off the ledge and let it bump on down the mountain. Or he knew I was there, had followed me, and just for pure meanness was going to shoot me in cold blood, after making me wait. Either way, my body would be destined for a bumpy roll down the side of the mountain.

My only hope was to hold still as stone and pray he hadn't seen me and would aim his gun in another direction.

Suddenly, I heard music and shifted my eyes back to him where he sat on the saw horse. I hadn't even realized I had, by nature, been looking around, searching for a way out.

Cherokee was holding what I had thought was a gun

to his mouth. *A harmonica,* I said to myself, and for the first time my chest let go enough to admit air sufficient to survive.

And that boy wasn't a beginner, either. He didn't play random notes. He began by playing the mountain hymn, "On Top of Old Smoky." I reckon every mountain person learns that before they learn their ABC's. Then he branched off and spun out "Down in the Valley" and "The Shucking of the Corn."

I thought to goodness he'd stop there. But, no. He flew into a couple of fast ones, beating out rhythm with his foot hanging down. Talk about lively! That boy burned the air with his music.

How did a half-breed from Davis Bottoms come to know such songs, I wondered.

I was beginning to get antsy because that pre-dark feeling was sinking around the sawmill and I knew night wasn't too far away. Then I'd have to make a decision. Was I scareder of nighttime or of Cherokee Fish, who had near murdered a white boy in cold blood in front of forty-seven witnesses?

I had just come to an answer when the music stopped. Cherokee Fish pulled himself off the sawhorse, careful not to snag a splinter, and pocketed the harmonica. Then he plunged back into the woods the way he came.

Why doesn't he use the path like a normal person, I wondered.

I waited a long time to give him space to get wherever he was heading. I had already decided I'd rather bump into the dark than that boy. So I sat there waiting for him and his music to go.

The stones across the creek were slick and I could hardly make them out, so much darkness was settling. I hurried, but was careful to test each step before I left the last one behind. All I needed to make my panic complete was to skid off into that cold creek. By the path, it wasn't but about five minutes to my front porch. Mama had already flipped on the front-porch light. I could see it shining yellow before I left the path. She had bought it on special at the Piggly Wiggly. I had been with her and seen the sign.

"Look, Mama," I had told her. "Bug lights."

"All electric light bulbs are bug lights," she had said, heading around the display.

"No, but look. These are new. They keep the bugs *away*," I told her.

She slowed. Stopped. Looked back at the sign. "All right. But just one . . . "

"But they come in lots of two," I had yelled after her as she started off again.

"Two then," she had called out as she disappeared down the Ritz Crackers aisle.

I noticed there weren't many bugs this evening as I came up on the porch. Two or three tiny ones zigzagging an orbit. Not the crowds of them that used to come out of the darkness to circle and die.

The smile I felt because I had showed Mama something she didn't already know didn't last long. Before I started down the long hall connecting the living room to the dining room and kitchen, I could hear Mama and Daddy arguing. Sharp. Before the words were plain, the anger was.

"What in the Sam Hill were you doing at Truitt's Grocery in the first place?" Daddy was asking Mama as I came through the hall, passing into the dining room.

"Because," Mama stormed, "because Frank Truitt is the best butcher in town. I shop my groceries at Piggly Wiggly and my meat at —"

"Well, Helen, don't. Just don't go there anymore," Daddy interrupted her to say.

"You don't have any cause to shout at me, Horace Houp!"

I had stopped in the kitchen doorway, watching. She was stirring okra browning in a fry pan. He was drying his hands on a paper towel.

"I've had enough heaped on me without *your* shouting," she said. "There I was, walking in the door to Truitt's and all those women shopping snapped to attention like Dwight David Eisenhower had just entered the store. Before the screen door slammed shut behind me, there was a silence heavier than a plague."

Mama clamped her mouth shut and looked down at the okra hissing in the pan.

"And that's *my* fault?" Daddy asked, punching his tight-wadded paper towel into the trash can.

"Yes, it's your fault," she whipped out. "You stood in church and opened the biggest can of worms you ever did see. Talking big about integrating Vacation Bible School. What difference does it make to you, Horace? Answer me that. Jonah and Edie are too old to attend anymore."

I could hear the kitchen clock keeping time to the silence that came.

But before Daddy could answer, Mama came at him again. "I don't see you inviting those people home with you or out to lunch. You got one friend who's Indian? Tell me that."

Mama may have slipped her hand in Daddy's the night of the big fight at church, and given in and let me get two bug lights at the Piggly Wiggly, but she wasn't backing down one step from Daddy on this integration thing, now that it had stung her personally. She hadn't just changed her tune. She had changed her whole song.

"There I was, though," she went on, stirring and talking. "I got my cutlets and two pounds of ground round and walked on up to the cash register, mindful of the looks my back was collecting. If they'd of been tangible, I'd of been covered up with the stares those women were passing out.

"Here's Miz Truitt at the cash register, solemn as a brick chimney. No reading that woman's face, so I had no preparation for what was coming."

"I don't want to hear this," Daddy said, but seeing me in the door frame to the dining room, he stopped where he stood.

Mama went on. "She says, 'That'll be three thirty-nine,' and I say, 'Just put it on my tab,' and she says, 'From now on, Miz Houp, it'll have to be cash on the barrel.' 'Cash on the barrel?' I ask, still not getting the picture. 'Cash on the barrel,' she says again like I was hard of hearing, and looked over to where Mr. Truitt was standing behind the butcher counter.

"Then I hear a snicker from behind me over at the Wonder Bread aisle. And it comes together in my mind. 'Because my husband thinks he wants to do right by the Indians, you mean?' I ask her.

"She doesn't answer. Just looks at her big freckled hands lying on the counter like two peanut-butter bars.

"'That's just fine with me,' I tell her and thank the good Lord I had the money on me. 'I've been meaning to check out Piggly Wiggly's meats,' I say. 'Only reason I came here was because I felt sorry that Piggly Wiggly has sucked up all your business.'

"I plopped that money down, collected my change, and yanked up my bald meats. Left her standing there, shaking out a paper sack to put them in. And it's all *your* doing, Horace Houp."

Boy! Mama didn't so much as draw a breath between telling what happened and fastening the blame on Daddy.

Supper was quiet. I knew Gramma had heard them yelling. I watched her chase her fried okra round her plate and wondered how she was feeling, trapped in a house with two people mad enough to kill each other, like I was trapped. And Jonah.

Mama had this kitchen radio up high on a shelf Daddy made for her. Even painted the shelf apple green like the rest of the kitchen. She listened to her country music while she cooked. Usually, the last person to sit for supper reached up and snapped it off. This night, though, that radio played right on through, and welcome to the noise. It was better than silence split with sounds of forks sliding on plates.

I knew what Mama was saying. We were all feeling the echoes of what Daddy had said that Wednesday night in church. I wondered if he was slipping through the days at the hardware store he managed without one person acting different toward him. Maybe he didn't tell us and they really were. If they weren't, it wasn't right because *he* was the one who said it and we were the ones who were absorbing all the anger from it.

Later, I lay in the dark on my cot, listening. The house was quiet save for low music coming under the crack of Jonah's door. Mama and Daddy's light was off, and nothing but darkness from under their door. I looked before I lay down.

I could hear tree frogs rasping out my open windows and the creek like rain, running down the mountain. I started in wondering where the creek came from and where it finally went to after it left us. I knew it passed into Lake Dew down toward town. But after that I never saw it. It went somewhere. Did it go into town,

I wondered. Did it travel as far as Davis Bottoms, where the half-breeds lived, past the shacks down there? Past the little houses built with spaces between the up-and-down boards where you could see people moving in the light inside. Jonah had told me about them. Did Cherokee Fish hear the creek, I wondered. When he couldn't make his own music, did he listen to the music the creek made?

5

When there's a feud going, it affects the people around it, on the edges. Mama and Daddy normally didn't let a week go by that they didn't feud about something. But this was the biggest feud ever, and it was contagious. Like chicken pox. The very next morning at breakfast, me and Jonah got into the worst ruction ever. And over nothing. It was just because our hackles were up, and we snapped before we even knew it.

Mama heard us and came rushing into the kitchen like a policeman. "What are you two arguing about?" she asked, her hands raising up to her hips, where she parked them, waiting for an answer.

"Edie Jo says . . . ," Jonah started and then stopped to laugh and slap the table.

"Well?" Mama said, not amused. Whatever the opposite of *amused* is, that was what she was. Unamused.

That didn't choke Jonah off any, though. He sat there and threw his head back and roared. Stomped his foot up and down. But, through all that, he had his sights on Mama, because when the very first inkling of her getting tired of standing there came, he wound right down and spoke up.

"Edie Jo says that service stations have got something new now. She says they have electric commodes. Electric commodes!" And he started in again.

"They do. Don't they, Mama?" I asked, sure she would back me up.

"I never heard of such," she said, going over and pouring herself some coffee.

"See, Hot Shot," Jonah said. "What'd I tell you."

That made me madder than ever. "There are so electric commodes," I said loud. "I've used them."

Jonah strangled on his Rice Krispies and I was glad because then maybe I could talk.

"They're at service stations. The seat part . . ."

"The counter," Mama said, stirring her milk into her coffee.

". . . the counter is folded up inside a shell with an electric blue light glowing. It sanitizes the seat . . ."

"Sterilizes," Mama said.

"Maybe they don't have them in boys' bathrooms because boys don't sit. They stand."

Jonah stood up and brayed out another laugh.

"She's right," Mama said. "They are electric."

Finally!

Jonah stopped in the middle of his laugh. He did this all the time. I guess it caught people with a stupid grin on their face and he suddenly went solemn and there you sat.

He looked at me and Mama and said, "I'm adopted. Please tell me I'm adopted."

He left, crossing the dining room, bumping into Daddy as he went. "Don't go in there," Jonah warned him. "They're talking about electric commodes."

"Electric commodes?" Daddy asked as he came in the door. "What's he talking about?"

Most days, after a feud, Mama would have leveled her head and looked at something out the window, but a smile would have played around her mouth and he'd have come over and touched her shoulder. She never could stay mad at Daddy long.

But not this day. She got up and took her coffee and left, went out to the back porch and on outside into the yard. Couldn't even stand to be in the same house, I reckoned.

I just ate along on my Cheerios and eyed the bowl of stewed prunes sitting in a glass dish in the middle of the table. Finally, I reached over and fished out a cooked lemon slice and ate it.

"That doesn't count," Daddy said. Serious.

"I know," I said and ate a prune.

Gramma came shuffling in, her bathrobe tied up against the morning chill. She poured herself some coffee and sat to the table.

"Mother," Daddy said, "did you sleep well?" Then, without even waiting for her answer, he said, "Mother, I need to go over this again with you and be sure you don't recall having a run-in with anybody just before the fire." Not "Have a bowl of cereal" or even "Have a prune." Just *bingo!* Back to the fire.

She looked up at him. Then shook her head.

"Well," Daddy went on, "Sheriff Stringfield asked me to get you to keep thinking on that. Keep trying to remember if you have any enemies that you know of."

She shook her head again. "Why do you keep asking me that?"

"Well," Daddy answered her, "seems like they are convinced this fire was set on purpose. And folks don't just go round setting fires," he frowned at the thought, "to watch houses burn. They usually have a reason."

Gramma sat and stared at the green oilcoth table cover. I worked the prune pit to one side of my mouth and watched her. When she looked up at my daddy, her eyes brimmed over with tears and she quick pressed her napkin to her mouth to hold in her grief.

I looked over at Daddy and he motioned me out with his head. I parked the prune pit on my napkin and left for the back porch. Standing just inside the porch, I was hid but I could hear Gramma crying and Daddy giving her comfort. I looked out into the yard and saw Mama standing near the clotheslines, watching the creek like it was the *Movie Tone News of the Week* at the picture show.

A feud is an awesome and awful thing. I wondered

did a feud start my gramma's fire. I wondered where this feud would lead to.

That afternoon, Mary Grady came home with me after school. It coming up a weekend, I had asked Mama and she had said yes. That was before the feud festered and burst. Friday morning was too late to do anything about it. Mary Grady was eating supper with us, too, before she went home. No spending the night anymore because we were pushing out the sides of the house with just the five of us. I wondered how supper was going to work out, but I decided the chips would have to fall where they fell.

Mary Grady and I went to the creek right after we got off the school bus at the top of the driveway. Took off our shoes and socks and were squealing at the coldness of the water when Jonah and David King, a friend of his, came out on the front porch. Jonah took the steps in one ripple. He could fly down steps faster than anybody I ever saw because he was so loose in his joints. He got in the car and backed it around. Waited until he got halfway up the drive to roll down his car window and yell to me, "D'ya tell Mary Grady about them electric commodes, Hot Shot?"

"About what?" she asked me, not believing he'd yelled out *commodes*.

I told her and she fell off the bridge laughing.

"It was a feud," I told her, "between Jonah and me. Everybody in my house is feuding. We're electric with feuds."

"What're all you feuding about?" she asked.

"Everything. You get in a mode of fighting and it's hard to let go. It's like a habit. Mama snaps at Daddy, then he snaps back. I yell at Jonah and he hollers back."

"What about?"

I shook my head. "It begun with integration. Now it's about anything that comes up. Do you believe in integration?" I asked her.

She looked over at me. "Who, me?"

"Who else is there?" I asked.

"I don't know. My mama don't."

"I didn't ask if your mama believed in it. I asked did you."

When Mary Grady closed her mouth, you could see the bumps her teeth made under her lip. She was saving for braces, she told me once. I watched her sitting there, her mouth tight over her bumpy teeth.

"I don't hate colored people," she said finally. "I don't know any."

"How about Indians?"

"Don't know any of them neither. Very good. Do you?"

I shook my head no. "Been in school with them all my life but never felt the urge to know any. Jonah says the Indian men come in town on Saturdays to sell their white lightning and the girls come to see can they pick up a white boy."

Mary Grady laughed. "What white boy in this town would be worth picking up? Maybe over to Asheville, but not in Half Moon."

· 43 ·

She picked up a mica stone and began peeling back the layers of mica with her fingernail. "Though I guess I hate them for what they did to me once."

I looked up at her and waited.

"Nobody in our family had ever had a new bike," she went on. "Used ones, yes, but not a brand-spanking-new one. Being as I was the youngest, everybody pitched in their bikes on a trade-in for a new bike for my ninth birthday . . ."

"I remember that," I said. "And you had it a week and somebody stole it."

"A Indian stole it. I saw him rounding the corner of the house on his way out. I hollered my head off but he hopped on it and took off. Never saw it again."

"I remember," I said.

"My daddy took me in the car that evening and we rode all through Davis Bottoms looking for that red and white Schwinn." She shook her head. "Nothing. Nowhere!"

We were quiet while she worked on the rock. Finally, I said, "But it was only one person who took it. One Indian. That don't mean all of them are thieves, just because one —"

"Let it be your bike." She stood and hurled the rock down the creek. "It don't matter if it's one or the whole Cherokee nation that took it. It was the only bike I ever got and it's gone."

As we were walking back to the edge of the creek to dig for crayfish, she added, "I still look for it sometimes."

I watched the water in the creek making its ripples

around rocks, always changing, moving, steady. "I really don't know," I told her, "how I feel about them, since they've never done anything to me, personally. They scare me because they're different, but I don't guess I hate them." I came alongside her. "Not yet, anyway."

"Why'd you say it like that?" she asked. "Like you don't now, but you may soon?"

I shook my head. "I'd be afraid to like them. Afraid of what people would do to somebody who had a friend who was a Indian.

"I've seen what they're doing to my family and we don't even know any Indians. Not personally. All my daddy did was stand up in church and say Vacation Bible School needs to be integrated. People all over town stopped talking to us. Stopped being friends."

"I didn't," she said quick.

I smiled at her and she smiled back.

"You ever been inside a Indian's house?" she asked in a minute.

I shook my head.

"How about a colored person's?"

I nodded.

"Who?" she asked.

"Hezekiah's wife died and me and Mama went up to their house on Falmouth Road to take food. Hezekiah had helped out when Grandpa was so sick, and Mama said she'd never forget it. And she didn't. We sat on the porch with Hezekiah —"

"That don't count. You weren't inside —"

"Yes, I was," I snapped. "Went clean through to the kitchen."

"Clean through to the kitchen?"

I ignored her echoing. It was just her way, I figured.

"Was the house any different from ours?" she asked me. "Hezekiah's?"

I shook my head, remembering photographs on walls and a wood stove in the kitchen radiating heat like it was the sun itself. Then I changed my mind and started nodding.

"Which is it?" she said. "Yes, it's different? No, it's not?"

"Yes, it was different. More people. No wallpaper. No flowers. Wood cooking stove."

"Different, then," she said.

I thought on that. Nodded. "Comfortable," I told her. "A lot happier than my house now with all the feuding. At least, Hezekiah's was."

"Oh, everybody's house has feuding in it . . ."

"Yes, but that house had people who laughed now and then. They cried some, too. But even at a funeral time they were laughing. Seems to me my house hasn't seen a laugh in months, if you don't count Jonah making fun of me."

I wanted to tell her more about the feuding, about my gramma crying, about Cherokee Fish playing the harmonica and making music you never dreamed of. But I held back. Sometimes, when you tell a person something, it doesn't belong to you anymore.

6

That evening at supper, Jonah tried to liven things up. We ate in the dining room. The first time since Christmas. Mary Grady and I lit the candles on the table, and Jonah cracked jokes and kept the talk hopping. It passed okay.

"Hot Shot, how about I take Mary Grady home?" Jonah said as we were clearing the table. "No need for Mama to have to drive her."

I had hoped she could stay longer. It was only going on seven-thirty. If Gramma didn't have my room, I thought afresh, Mary Grady could have spent the night. That thought didn't do much for my frame of mind.

"I'll ask Mama," he said, heading for the kitchen. I guess my silence had been read a way he wanted to read it.

"Only if I get to ride, too," I walked into the kitchen to say.

Jonah frowned, but Mama agreed.

We were lost, me and Mary Grady, in the back seat of our 'fifty-four Chevy. Four other people could have sat in there comfortable. After we deposited Mary Grady at her house, I moved on up to the front beside Jonah.

"Where we going?" I asked above Elvis growling on the radio when he turned off the main road and headed down a street I'd never been on before.

"Just riding," he said, sticking his arm out his open window.

"I want to ask you something," I said. "How come you to know what them shacks in Davis Bottoms look like?"

He was working on a toothpick. He took it out and spit out the window. Wiped his mouth on his shirt shoulder. Stuck the toothpick back in his mouth. Did all this before he answered me.

"I pass 'em now and then, when I'm in that neck of the woods. They're just on the other side of the mountain from our house."

"Why would you ever be in that neck of the woods?" I asked, interested. I'd never been down into Davis Bottoms.

"My girl lives up Raymer Road and you have to drive by Davis Bottoms to get there. Why?" He looked over at me. I kept my eyes casual on the houses we were passing. I didn't even know he had a girl. But I had seen "Emily" written on the side of a schoolbook he carried. I should have known.

"Just wondered," I said, stretching and yawning to underscore how casual a question it was. It *was* casual. I didn't care, just curious.

"Is she half-breed?" I asked, because if she lived that close to Davis Bottoms, she might be. Boy! Talk about a fit. We hadn't seen anything yet if Mama found out Jonah was dating an Indian girl.

"Lord no," Jonah said. "She doesn't live in Davis Bottoms. I didn't say that. She lives up Raymer Road on a little farm.

"We're passing some of them shacks now," he said, pointing over to the right. "See there yonder, down that street."

I looked. Jonah had slowed for a stop sign. I could see the houses good. Light came out in the spaces between those up-and-down boards like they were thin slips of cellophane or mica. Glowing in the dark. We weren't close enough to make out people moving, but I could see colors passing around.

"Davis Bottoms," Jonah said and belched for punctuation.

He turned right at a street at the foot of a hill. The houses stopped and fields began to edge the road.

"Where we going now?" I asked.

"Just checking to see if my girl's home yet. She told me she had to do some shopping in Asheville. Just checking."

He wasn't fooling me. He had planned to go to her house all along. If I hadn't given him a good excuse with taking Mary Grady home, he would have had to ride his bicycle.

We had slowed coming up on a stop sign and were

leaning to turn left when movement from both sides of the road caused Jonah to slam on the brakes. I nearly rammed into the windshield, it was so sudden.

A bunch of boys, four or five, lunged at the car from the sides of the road, banging with their fists and slapping with the flats of their hands on the fenders and hood and shouting and yelling. The noise was like a bonfire it was so hot.

"Oh-oh-oh-oh! What have we here?" one tall one said and leaned on my window. My half-open window. He looked in at me. "I think I caught me a little girl," he whispered. I could tell he was one of the half-breeds. Not Cherokee Fish, though. Still the same blue-black hair and the smooth skin color. But this boy's face was so near it was like looking in a mirror only it was him, not me, staring at my face.

"What d'you know?" he said, sort of high for a boy.

"Drive, Jonah!" I yelled, hammering the door lock down.

But the window being part open, it wasn't anything for him to just lift the lock back up. He did.

"Drive!" I screamed.

Jonah tried. But the bodies out front had crawled onto the hood and blocked his view.

"Jesus Christ!" Jonah hissed.

"What's your name?" the boy at my window whispered. He reached through and silked down my hair. I could feel the hairs on the back of my neck stand straight out. He smiled like I was to enjoy him handling my hair as much as he was.

That smile did it. When I was six years old I got sick for the first time in my life and vomited. That kept up more regular than not for three years before it quit and I came to feel I'd rather be dead than throwing up. That same feeling swept all through me. I coughed and retched and screamed at the same time and crawled toward Jonah, but those hands through the window were hard and strong.

Jonah threw the car in reverse and floored it. We began to spin our tires. Then, without warning, the car suddenly shot backwards. It swerved from where Jonah had begun to make the turn and he straightened it fast. We kept going back. Straight up the road we had driven down.

"Roll up your window and close that little front one! Lock your door quick!" Jonah was yelling and fixing his own windows. "Reach around and lock the back doors!"

I half expected to see a pair of arms, broken off, still through my window. But I guessed he had gotten out with both his arms.

When we got to a cross street, Jonah backed into it and threw the car into first. I looked where we had come from and saw them in the moonlight, all crouched. Watching.

Jonah floored it to get us out of there. And that's when it happened. The car died. Choked.

"Damn! Damn! Damn!" Jonah screamed. He banged his forehead on the steering wheel with each word.

"Turn off the lights so the battery won't drain," I said, remembering when Daddy had stalled once. My hands became the knots I could feel inside my stomach.

Jonah killed the lights and I looked back down the street. They were all gone. Every last one of them.

"Whew!" I breathed in a shaky voice. "They've done gone."

Jonah looked, too, but I didn't hear any sigh of relief coming from his direction.

"They're gone from view, all right," he whispered. "They're Indians, Hot Shot. They ain't gone far. They're stalking us."

The terror I had let out flooded back in. We didn't stand a chance. There weren't any houses near us. Just some fields and houses further on back.

Jonah ground and ground that starter. I guessed my job was to watch. I couldn't figure where we'd be seeing them come from, so I tried to cover all sides in a pretty regular sweep, like a big searchlight on a rocky coast. Like it was going to do any good! What would we do different if we were to see them? But it gave me something to do while Jonah pumped the accelerator, then ground the starter.

And then he just quit.

"We have to give it a minute," he whispered, like they were going to be listening to what all we said. "It'll rejuvenate itself on its own. I've flooded it. I hope to God we've *got* a minute."

I knew they'd be mad, seeing as how we left bodies rolling around, we flew out of there so fast. Not a one of them was going to be in a good mood. It was stupid, but all I could think of was that quote in history class, what the Japanese commander said after he set off the attack on Pearl Harbor. Something about being afraid he had awakened a sleeping giant.

"There," Jonah said low.

"Where?" I asked, looking at him to see where he was looking.

"There by that big tree just off the road. See? See the hands on either side."

I could have closed my eyes and sworn I was in our yard and Jonah was giving his careful lessons on being afraid of the dark. But we were here and the dark might turn out to be the best friend we had. It was the least of our worries, anyway.

"Try the car again," I begged, forgetting to whisper.

Jonah wiped his forehead on his shoulder and whispered, "Please, dear God, let this bastard start!"

I'd never heard Jonah say that word before. Only seen it written on the walls of bathroom stalls, surrounding those electric commodes. The word was electric itself, and awful. But it must have waked up God, because that engine purred into power like an airplane setting off down an open runway.

Jonah never batted an eye. He took off out of there, and sorry for you if you were in the way. I tried to look back and see if they were still there, but when we left, the dark filled the street and I couldn't tell.

We didn't tell anybody about that night, Jonah and me.

"Hot Shot, we gotta keep this to ourselves," he told me when we turned down our driveway off the main road. "It won't take much to push Mama and Daddy into clamping down on us tight. Do, and we might never see daylight again. They're mad enough at each other as it is, over this racial thing. God only knows what they might do if they found out about this. You and me might have to hire bodyguards to ever get out of Houp Holler."

When we got out of the car, Jonah felt all over the hood and front fenders for dents their fists might have made.

"What you looking at, son?" a voice called out from the dark front porch. When I quick looked up, I could see the raw end of my daddy's cigarette glowing in the dark.

"Nothing," Jonah called back, almost too fast. "I heard a rock fly up and hit someplace. Just checking."

He stooped to hide himself behind the car so he could warn me one last time. "Don't tell nothing! Understand? Nothing!"

"I won't," I said, low.

Even after everybody else had gone inside, me and Gramma sat there on the porch in the dark.

"Sit up next to me in the swing, Edie Jo," she said. "It's chilly out here."

I came over to her and found a place up close where I could feel her dress, coarse, rubbing me as we swung. Her arm was warm around my shoulder. But, to tell the truth, an eiderdown comforter couldn't have kept me warm that night. Something inside me had temporarily gone out. Like a pilot light. And I was cold from the inside out.

That night, in my corner bedroom, I wrote again in the empty book. When Mama gave it to me on my thirteenth birthday, she had written on the first page:

To Edie Jo

Hope your 13th year will be good. Here's an empty book for you to record your days in. I have the feeling that someday you'll be our writer so you best start now.

Love,
Mama

I kept the book in one of the Gerber baby-food boxes under my cot. I never did write accounts of things. That'd just be like an echo playing it back. What I did write were thoughts and poems about things. I wrote one poem about fog on a morning in September, right after I got the book. There were also several about what it would be like to be in love, a state I reckoned wasn't exactly as likely as fog.

That night me and Jonah were in the Bottoms I didn't write about fog or love. After the parts I had written about fear, I added something new. I put on paper *hate* and *terror*. I wrote that I'd decided integration was not for me. I hated people of color. All of them. I was afraid of them and I hated them.

7

A terror like me and Jonah came upon that night doesn't go anywhere. It clings to memory like the smell that doesn't leave a house once you've burned toast.

School let out for the summer. I was gladder than ever before because I didn't have to see that half-breed Fish boy and wonder if his friends came back to him that night and told him what all they did. And what all they nearly did.

Gramma and me were picking over black-eyed peas the first Monday afternoon of summer vacation. We were camped out on the front porch with a bottle of Coca-Cola each. It was a long job, so we made sure to be comfortable. Even took Mama's kitchen radio and set it on the floor of the porch just outside the door to the house. It had taken two extension cords to rig it up. We sorted peas while we listened to Gramma's favorite soap operas.

When *Young Dr. Malone* finished and a commercial came on, I up and asked Gramma what she felt about integration. Now that I'd made up my mind, I wondered how everybody else stood. I hadn't asked Jonah. Didn't need to, I reckoned, after our experience together. I already knew where Mama and where Daddy stood. Not together. All I knew about Gramma was that she hated arguing so bad she was willing to stand to the front of a church full of yelling people and sing at them. But I didn't know how she really felt.

"Integration?" she said, never missing a bad pea as she talked. "Well, I'll have to say, those folks are good in the sight of the Lord. He loves them, too. But I don't see nowhere in the Bible it says we're supposed to be intimate with them."

Gramma had a touch of the palsy and her head shook. I watched her bent over the black-eyed pea basin.

"Intimate?" I asked, not sure.

She frowned and looked up at me. "Close," she said, then sneezed seven times. It was her pattern. Everybody has a sneeze pattern. Hers was seven times. I counted under my breath and took a swig of Coke.

"Whew, Law!" she gasped. That always marked the end of her sneeze.

The opening for *Arthur Godfrey* cranked up. I dropped the little hard peas into the metal basin in time to the beat of the music.

"Edie Jo, you're not checking those close enough," Gramma said, stopping. "Slow down. Don't want any little stones or worms in with our peas."

"Yes, ma'am," I answered her. I slowed to being careful again, but I felt unsettled somehow. I had thought Gramma would have been *for* integration, not against it. After all, she had stood to the front of the church and sung "Turn Your Eyes upon Jesus." It was beginning to come clear to me that even people who said, "Let's have peace and live together like one big family," might not actually want to when it got down to the intimate part, as Gramma put it.

After we sorted all the peas, I took the good ones on back to Mama in the kitchen while Gramma waited for *Young Widder Brown* to come on. That was her favorite. I knew she'd be sitting out there until that finished up.

"Here now, Edie Jo," she called to me as I came back through the porch and started out the door to cross the front yard. "Where you think you're going?"

"For a walk," I hollered back. Sometimes it was like having two mamas, having a gramma and a mama.

"Don't you go too far now," she called out. "You hear?"

"Yes, ma'am," I called back and went up the narrow path to the sawmill. It'd been nearly two weeks since I'd been and had seen that Fish boy up there. I reckoned, now that school was let out, he'd probably hired out somewhere for the summer and it'd be safe to go back. It was my favorite place in Half Moon, and I wasn't going to let any half-breed keep me from it. I'd been going there off and on for a long time.

I went to my ledge and watched the cars and people below. It was like being God, looking down on the world. Reaching up, I ripped off two rhododendron leaves and tore slits in the middle of one, leaving the ends solid. Then I tore the other leaf into strips and wove them in and out the first leaf.

"It could make a coaster for a drink," I said out loud.

I decided to make five of them and decorate the table for supper. I sang "Turn Your Eyes upon Jesus" as I wove. I was on the fourth coaster when I thought I heard a voice from close by. I froze. Words hadn't reached me, only the sound of the voice.

Not moving my head, I looked with just my eyes. I didn't see anybody, and I was just thinking I had imagined the voice when it came again. I snapped my head to look across the clearing. What I saw was that Fish boy, standing on the far side of the creek. Watching me. Grinning.

"I said," he yelled out, "what'cha doing over there on the edge of space." I heard the words that time.

I felt my mouth clamp over my teeth the way Mary Grady's did when she was mad. The way I figured it, I had hemmed myself in good. Since I didn't have wings, the only way out was across the creek and right by him. I fought off the memory of that night me and Jonah like to got ourselves killed. This could be worse, a voice inside me warned.

I stood, and my coasters slid off my lap. One of them fluttered on down over the ledge.

Somehow, when I stood, it gave me strength. To this day I don't know where that strength came from, but

this voice from inside my body said, "I'm making coasters for the dinner table. And I'll thank you not to sneak
up on a person like that. It startled me."

I picked up the three coasters like I really cared about
them. They could have been gold with silver woven into
them the way I was acting.

"Coasters?" he asked.

I looked across at him. He had both hands stuck in
his jeans pockets. Same black T-shirt. Same shiny, black
hair. Cut maybe two months ago and needing a new cut
bad. And same half smile on his face.

"Coasters?" he repeated.

"I heard you the first time," that voice from inside
me said. Lord, where was it coming from? And why
was it being so lippy? He might not let me get as far as
the creek at this rate.

"They're like place mats. Only you put them under
your drinking glass," I said, starting toward the creek,
to cross.

"Place mats?" he asked now. I looked at him. His
eyebrows were frowned up like he really didn't know,
and he sort of leaned his head to one side to hear better.

"Bigger than these." I pointed to the coasters. "You
stick them under your plate to save the table top." I kept
walking.

"Miss Houp," he said.

"Why'd you call me that?" I asked, stopping short of
the creek.

"'Cause that's the name I remember. Old Miss Biggers either calls you 'people' or Miss or Mister whatever."

"My name's Edie Jo," I told him, stepping out on the first stone. He remembered me from class. Now at least he might understand why I'd not feel too friendly after what he'd done to Skeeter.

"I didn't think nobody ever came up here but me," he said.

Then whatever force had entered my body and carried me this far left me high and dry. Here I was, halfway across the creek, and suddenly I got the shakes and felt weak and trembly, thinking about all the times I'd come to the sawmill, all the years I'd been coming. Wondering if he'd seen me before.

"Oh, I see people up here all the time," I lied, answering him so fast he barely had his words past his mouth. My power-filled self would have waited and said it casual-like. But no, I blurted it out like my life depended on how quick those words would fly out of my mouth.

Knowing I did this, I lost my concentration and my foot slipped on the last rock. I shot toward the creek in a split second. But Cherokee lunged at me and yanked me toward him by my arm like I was a mountain trout he was netting for breakfast.

Thirteen years isn't normally the most poised age for a person, but I would have won an award for awkwardness. I sprawled in twelve different directions, nearly pulling him in with me. The rhododendron coasters went in the creek. It tells how strong he was that he pulled me and him out of there without both of us getting soaked.

"Whoo-wee!" he yelled, shaking off water I had kicked up. "What you trying to do? Pull me in that icy water alongside you?"

"I'm sorry," I sputtered, getting my balance back. "I slipped." I wiped mud off of one leg with the other foot.

"You should of seen yourself," he crowed like one of those barnyard roosters. Even whirled around once and strutted over to the sawhorse. "You and them skinny legs and arms flying every which a way. Lord help us! If I hadn't come along, you might of up and drowned yourself."

"I don't think so," I said, and I could feel my courage on the rise. Or maybe it was anger. His cocky attitude was enough to bring a saint down. "I've made it plenty of times by myself, thank you."

"You're very welcome," he said, settling himself on the back of the sawhorse.

I wondered was he going to pull out that harmonica and play a tune. The words to ask him were just forming when I remembered he hadn't known I was there that first time, and I stopped cold.

"Anytime one person in Half Moon can reach out and help another person in Half Moon, all the better, our fair town being a town of brotherly love." The sarcasm was a little soft because he still smiled.

"Ain't nothing wrong with Half Moon," I said, bracing one leg against a big boulder for support. I figured to talk a minute and sort of start backing away, saying my big brother had called me five minutes ago, that he'd be up here looking for me.

I was just congratulating myself on a good line to use when he said, "I been watching you for close onto ten, maybe even fifteen minutes. You'd better acquaint yourself with the ways of the woods, girl, 'fore the wrong person comes upon you out in the wilderness. You from here? I mean, as in *born here?*"

I nodded yes. "Born over to Buncombe County Hospital in Asheville, September 19, 1942." Good Lord, I thought, I open my mouth to say one thing and a whole trainful of words comes rolling out.

He hunched one shoulder at a time to pop his neck. I'd seen Jonah do it a thousand times. Then he asked, "You plan on living your whole life up here in these mountains? In the friendly town of Half Moon?"

I didn't know. It was a comfort to know I'd be having a life after all. Maybe he didn't mean me any harm.

"Grow up to be a skinny mountain woman," he kept on, "and get married and have a string of young'uns?"

He stopped. I realized he was waiting for my answer.

"Yes," I said, then, "No. I plan to go away to college and maybe come back here to live, maybe not . . ."

"In other words, your plans are subject to change," he said, nodding his head a little.

It makes me mad as fire when people put words in my mouth. If I had meant my plans were subject to change, that's what I would have said. "I'm not sure where I'll do it," I said, "but I know what I'm gonna be doing."

He lifted his eyebrows and blinked, waiting for me to go on.

"I'm gonna be a writer," I went on like God himself had inspired me to say it. I didn't know that for a fact. Just because Mama had said it since I read all the time didn't make it so. Seven poems do not a writer make. But suddenly I wanted to sound like I was in control of some part of my life. I certainly wasn't in control of my arms and legs.

"A writer?" he said, half question, half statement. He scratched his jaw, then smiled deeper and nodded again like he was looking into a crystal ball and saw me maybe not as a writer, but as an awkward, backward mountain person who would never leave Half Moon, maybe because she couldn't put one foot in front of the other without falling down.

"Me," he said suddenly, like I had asked him his plans, "I'm gonna get outta here the day I turn eighteen. I'll hike a train and head toward Raleigh or Charlotte. Get me some work where I can make fast bucks. Big bucks."

In the quiet that followed, I felt I'd probably need to say something back. "You ever coming back here?" I asked.

"Oh, maybe," he said. "Maybe one day I'll drive through town in a black Ford truck with gold stripes hand-painted round the fenders and a black lab riding along in the truck bed, barking at every no good son of a bitch we pass in this crummy town."

I began my backing up. Slow. The last thing I wanted was for him to start in mad. I'd seen the last time he got mad. No thank you.

"You know," he went on like I wasn't slowly backing away, like I wanted to hear everything he could tell me, "it's been one hell of a summer and it hasn't even started good yet. I took a job over at Atchison's farm for the summer, only it began back in April. Four-thirty of a morning till time for school to take in. Thought I'd pick me up some cash real fast. I figured working around them animals wouldn't be bad. Damn!" He shook his head.

I inched on backwards.

"Turned out to be hell on earth," he went on. "Feeding them baby cows of a morning. And birthing 'em. Jeez!" He looked to where the sky was supposed to be over top of the trees hiding it. "That turned out to be an experience I wouldn't want to repeat. Just last week a damn cow half-birthed her calf, then up and jumped to her feet and started wandering around that field like she was done and nothing left to do but flick flies off with her tail. I tried to get her to lay back down, but no."

I had stopped backing up, pictured in my mind the cow with the calf half hanging out of her.

"She took out running for all she was worth. Just about that time my manager drives up. He piles outta his truck and lights into me like a dog onto a cat. 'What you runnin' her for, you crazy half-breed!' he yells.

"'I'm trying to catch her,' I say, resting against a fence post to get my breath.

"'That ain't the way you do it,' he hollers. 'Fetch me that rope yonder in the back of my pickup.' I do and he lassoes her, but don't bump her down. Pulls hisself towards her and gentles her down and ties her feet together so she won't wander again. Then we take another rope and tie it around the front of the calf under the front legs. He ties the other end of the rope to the front bumper of the truck.

"'Now,' he tells me, 'you get yourself over there and help that calf come out while I pull.' He climbs into the cab and starts her up, gets in gear, and starts backing up real slow. The truck don't go nowhere for a while. Then suddenly, that calf starts coming out.

"'Slow down!' I holler at him so he don't yank that calf halfway round the county."

Cherokee stopped and looked off at the creek and just sat. Remembering. But his remembering wasn't doing me any good. I couldn't see the pictures in his head. "So?" I asked.

He blinked back to where we were and wiped his face with his hand. "Oh, that was it."

"Did the calf live?" I asked.

"Sure, sure. They're tough. Like I'm tough. You gotta be tough to survive in this world."

He sounded like a hundred-year-old man.

"So," he said, "I'm getting the hell away as soon as I can."

Jonah talked like that sometimes. Without the *hells* and all, though. He wouldn't live to walk ten feet if he used those words in front of Mama. And then I remembered what Mama told Jonah every chance she got. So, in place of saying I understood what he was feeling, which I should have said because I sort of did, Half Moon being what it was, I started in with Mama's speech about you can't get anywhere in this world without an education. Used to be, in her day, just a high school diploma was all you needed.

"Now it's a college degree," I told him. "And in the next twenty years, it'll be a graduate school degree." Like I knew what I was talking about.

He just looked at me. His swinging foot stopped. I had his attention, I knew, so I kept on rolling. While I was talking, he lifted himself off the sawhorse and started walking toward me. I began talking faster, thinking maybe if he was planning on attacking me he wouldn't if I was to keep on talking. As long as I talked, I was safe.

Finally, he stopping walking not a yard from me. He held up his hand for me to stop. Not once had his smile left his face. That really worried me. I'd read somewhere that murderers sometimes smile while they kill.

I stopped.

He didn't say anything. Just stood there looking at me. Finally, he started talking. So low I had to strain to hear.

"You are so far from where I am," he said, slow and in a voice the color of sky before a storm.

I just looked at him.

"Here you are, talking about graduate school, when I'm going to be doing well to make it through high school. Where do you come off talking about graduate school degrees anyhow? Your talk gives you away, Edie Jo. You talk like you're just from Half Moon, North Carolina, not New York. Not even Charlotte or Raleigh. You're about as pure mountain as a person can get.

"I'll tell you something," he said, getting louder. "You walk a mile in *my* moccasins, Kemosabe, before you start giving me lectures. Okay? You live at *my* house. With *my* old man. All right?"

He slapped a mosquito on his neck, but his eyes never wavered. "I'll tell you," he said, nodding his head, "you'd leave too, if you was me.

"Tell me something," he said, shifting gears and talking softer. "Have you ever been hungry? I mean really hungry? Have you ever spent whole months without eating a bar of candy or drinking a Coke? Ever known what it was like to steal a watermelon from a field by moonlight, knock it open on a rock, and eat it like it was the greatest dessert ever made? You know what it's like to eat potatoes for supper, and then again for breakfast? Every day?"

He sucked his mouth up tight like he'd done that day he attacked Skeeter, and he stood there looking at me. I watched him, knowing my life wasn't worth two cents.

Then he shifted and looked at the ground for a long time. When he looked back up, his eyes were different. I could tell something had passed on out of him.

"I didn't mean to holler at you," he said, lifting his head a little and smiling his half smile again. "I just don't cotton to sermons much."

He walked on past me and into the woods without saying another word. It was enough, though. His words were everywhere, all inside my head and inside the sawmill camp.

That night, Half Moon had its second fire, and this time the person who lived there didn't get off as easy as Gramma. It was Truitt's Grocery that burned and Mr. Truitt inside. Mrs. Truitt was off in Greensboro visiting her sister. But Mr. Truitt, asleep upstairs over his store, behind the windows with red geraniums in the window boxes — Mr. Truitt burned slam up. It took fire trucks from four neighboring communities to put out the blaze so it wouldn't set the next-door buildings on fire.

Daddy took us all into town when we heard the sirens. We rode down and parked on Second Street and watched it from the back of Daddy's store. I could feel the heat from where we stood. The same heat like when Gramma's house burned.

"A fire pure makes a person sick to their stomach," Mama said, slipping her arm around Gramma. Knowing she was remembering.

8

Where I come from, when somebody dies, the funeral doesn't take place right away. It's at least three days later. Sometimes four. In Mr. Truitt's case, the sheriff had to put in a call to Mrs. Truitt in Greensboro and she had to collect her wits, I guess, and then travel back. Mr. Truitt died on a Monday night and his funeral took place on the following Thursday. In between time, every woman in town worth her salt was cooking up cakes and stirring congealed salads and shredding fresh coconut into ambrosia and showing up at Mrs. Truitt's pastor's house, where she was temporarily staying since she didn't have a home anymore.

Mama sent Jonah to the Piggly Wiggly to buy some milk and things and a dozen eggs for a ten-egg pound cake to take to Mrs. Truitt. Jonah and his friend David King came driving down our driveway a half hour later with Mama's groceries in the trunk. Jonah grabbed all the sacks but one.

"Get them eggs, will you, David?" he said, nodding his head at the last sack.

I've got to say, to be so good-looking, David King had about the brains of an egg. I watched from where I stood on the front steps, holding the porch door wide for them. David picked up the sack with the dozen eggs in it and closed the trunk. Then, he headed in my direction to bring those eggs in to Mama.

All was fine and well. I was just noticing how his shoulders were wide as a yard measuring stick when he sees me watching him. So he grins big. Then he takes and flips that sack with that cardboard carton right straight up in the air and catches it like he's picking off a pop-up in the Yankee outfield.

I grin. Big.

"Wanna see me do it behind my back?" he calls.

Why not, I think. *We're all living dangerous these days.* I nod.

So he whaps those eggs up into the air again, even higher, steps forward to catch them behind his back, and stumbles over a stone the size of a person's hand. Those eggs sail right down behind him, passing him going ninety miles an hour, but he's too busy hanging on to a standing position to reach out and grab them.

The sack lay on the ground where it had hit, like a small dead body.

"Oh, no," he whispered.

Eggs were high priced. Twenty-nine cents a dozen wasn't something to sneeze at.

He picked up the sack gentle as if it were a baby

and moved fast for the kitchen. That sack was already staining.

"It'll just be a twelve-egg pound cake," Mama said, not perturbed. "I'll add more flour." She probably thought he'd tripped coming up the steps. After all, he'd been trying to help out. But let that be Jonah or me and we'd have caught an earful.

David King had come over right often that spring, since Jonah could borrow our car and David's family didn't own one. He even went to the funeral with us Thursday. And to the cemetery after.

"Why are we going?" I asked Mama from where I sat in the middle of the front seat. "Mrs. Truitt was ugly to you and you don't shop their store no more."

Mama lifted her chin and watched out the windshield. It was still a subject she wasn't enthusiastic about discussing. Finally, she said, "Death changes things and you're willing to be more charitable."

I looked over at Daddy, but he just drove. So, if Daddy were to die, I thought, maybe Mama would start speaking to him again. I thought about what Mama said the rest of the way to the cemetery and for a long time afterward.

At the cemetery McLean's Funeral Parlor had set up a blue tent without sides, in case it rained, I guessed. It sure wasn't to shade you from the sun. Trees the size of mammoths stood over us, their big-knuckled roots bulging up above the ground. I watched my step, not wanting to pull a David King and trip myself.

Daddy and Jonah and David stood over to the side of where we sat, to leave chairs for the ladies. Every so often I looked over at Jonah and David to see that they hadn't snuck off.

When the graveside service was done, we picked our way between the roots to get out of the cemetery. Seemed like planting a person was a perfectly natural thing, I thought. Where else were you going to put them? I watched Mrs. Truitt being helped to her car. She was mighty broken up. We passed her, not farther than a couple of yards, and I could hear her sobbing out loud.

It's really strange to walk right past a person who's turning inside out with hurting and you not feel a thing. It's like sitting in the picture show for the *Movie Tone News* and watching a hurricane burst through a place but not feel the wind and rain. Just see it. Protected.

I began to wonder if something was missing inside me. Maybe, like a person who was born blind, I was born without some feelings. Feelings like sympathy for a person suffering, like Mrs. Truitt and Gramma. Like for Cherokee being so poor he'd steal a watermelon.

One thought led to another. I began to wonder if maybe I wouldn't ever be able to feel other things, like love for a boy, either. So far, I hadn't felt anything. Those poems I had written about love weren't connecting me to the real thing. I was thirteen years old. Going close on fourteen. And nothing.

And thinking it made it so. I decided I had definitely been born missing.

Mama's answer about a death causing a person to be more charitable still bothered me. I wanted to know what Daddy had to say so maybe I'd understand why one minute you can be mad as fire at a person, mad to the extent you won't trade at their store anymore; then, let them die, and suddenly you're bringing food to their widow, acting like nothing ever happened in the first place.

I thought about that all through the first week of June. One evening in June when it was just warm enough to sit outside without a jacket and daylight was beginning to hang around longer and longer, I saw Daddy sitting in a rocker on the front porch right by himself, and so I went on out.

"When are we going to get a television set, Daddy?" I asked as I plopped down in the porch swing.

"Not just yet," he said.

"You can't say, 'Wait and see if it catches on' no more," I told him.

He didn't say anything. I figured getting television was still a dead-end street.

Finally, after we'd sat awhile, I asked him what was really on my mind. "Daddy, how come Mama took a pound cake to Mrs. Truitt when they hate each other?"

He dragged on his cigarette and blew smoke. "Edie

Jo, your mama was hurt. I think by taking the cake over she was trying to say, 'Let's put this behind us and move on.'"

I swung awhile, then asked him, "When's the rest of the town going to put this behind them? In church it's as cold as the inside of our Frigidaire. All them people hate us, Daddy. All because of what you said. And it got voted down anyhow. So only white kids are going to wind up going to Vacation Bible School. And the worst part?" I said, bringing the swing to a stop it made me so mad. "The worst part of all is them Indians don't even know to thank you. It was like throwing fifty cents down a deep hole. You said it for nothing."

In the quiet, I could hear our creek running to wherever it went. A car flashed by at the top of the drive. Still we sat.

Finally Daddy took a deep breath. "Edie Jo, sometimes a person is given the opportunity to do something right, to stand for something. It don't happen every day. When that doorway opens, you gotta go through it or be forever looking back, wishing you had."

I looked at him sitting there, his white shirtsleeves rolled up to his elbows, his dark hair still in place, plastered there by the palmful of Vitalis he soaked on it of a morning.

"But did you have to go and drag the rest of us through the door with you?" I asked him. His eyes raised to look at me, and I knew at once I had hurt him. And I honestly didn't care, once more proving how I was born missing some of my feelings.

Late that evening, when dark had swung itself clean through Houp Holler, I went out to the back porch to down a tumbler of milk and see if I could spy Orion's belt up in the sky. It was the only constellation I could ever identify with certainty, and, the stars being like fish in an ocean, it was a comfort to set my sights on one part of my world that stayed familiar.

As I stood looking through the screened in upper part of the porch wall, I ran my hand over Mama's smooth whetstone. She had been sharpening knives on that stone since before I was born. Maybe it was as old as the stars, I was thinking when, slow as a full moon rising, there came up right in front of me at the screen a face. Its shiny forehead caught what little moonlight there was and reflected it like waxed linoleum. That and the whites of the eyes were all I could focus on.

My voice was the first part of me to come alive. It wrenched a scream out long before my arms and legs rose to the occasion. By the time I began backing away and my scream had reached around through the house to collect everybody still up, the face had swallowed itself back into the night.

Daddy even called Sheriff Stringfield. He came over and they searched around the yard for over an hour. Mama and I helped look, too, and I was thinking about waking Gramma and Jonah to come help when the sheriff called a halt.

"Horace," he told Daddy, "I don't see nothing out of order. No bushes trampled. No tracks."

They had crisscrossed the yard with their flashlight beams, searching for something to say who had been there and just left.

"You sure your little girl didn't imagine this whole thing?" Sheriff Stringfield asked Daddy.

Maybe it was just the question, pure and simple, but I was betting it was more than that. I was betting it was the fires. I was betting it was my words to Daddy about dragging us all into his fizzled integration crusade. I was betting it was all those things that made Daddy turn on the sheriff like a pit bull.

"Hell no, she didn't imagine it!" he shouted, standing there in the back yard with his blue pajama bottoms hanging below his bathrobe. "No more than we imagined the fire that ate up my mother's house and all she had in this world.

"When is the Sheriff's Department going to get a move on and unearth something substantial in this so-called investigation of arson? The whole damn town going to have to burn like Rome while you fiddle away, playing Nero?"

My daddy's question hung in the air like a person's breath on a cold night.

The sheriff stood with his legs bowed back, bracing against the world, I reckoned. "You are one contentious son of a bitch, Horace Houp," he growled low so me and Mama wouldn't hear. But we did.

"You bet," Daddy whipped out. "You bet I am when it comes to my family's safety being at stake." He tilted his head to one side, still glaring at Sheriff Stringfield. "I'm counting on you, Sheriff. I'm counting on you to find some more of what you refer to as 'calling cards' and to make some sense out of them and solve these crimes. Time's passing and I don't see any progress. None at all!"

He punched those last three words out like he was sending a telegram. I was sure Sheriff Stringfield got the telegram by the way he took off out of there, all surly and tight.

I watched his headlights make two spokes upward in the driveway as he drove off. Then I watched my mama and daddy go inside and into their bedroom. I watched the path of light under their door disappear. Then I watched the luminous hands of the clock take the night down, one hour at a time. It was hazing up dawn out my windows and the stars were sinking back into the sky the last time I looked before I finally found sleep. And then heavy sleep didn't start in until the comfort of people sounds played like a lullaby and I let go my silent watch for the face I had seen.

9

When I woke up, my clock said eleven-forty. The smell of fried ham and coffee was fading. Then, when I put my feet to the floor, I felt like I hadn't slept more than a couple of hours.

I took a long, soaking bath and powdered talc on myself till there was a fine layer of white coating on the toothbrushes and combs and all in the bathroom. I took a bowl of Cheerios out to the front porch and sat with Gramma.

"Did you hear about the face I saw at the back porch last night?" I asked her right off the bat.

"I heard," she said.

Well, good grief! I had expected more. After all, I could have been killed dead, and all she said was, "I heard."

I watched her to see if there'd be more. But that was it. I figured she'd been through so much, nothing was ever going to faze her again. Not even near death, much less faces in the night.

"What you doing?" I asked her finally. She was working with some near-white string. "You going to tie up something with that string?" I asked.

She shook her head. "No," she said. "I went out and bought myself some thread and I'm going to crochet something beautiful."

"Why?" I asked. Actually, I guess what I meant was, why was she going to crochet? A person wouldn't set out to crochet something ugly.

"Because," she said, laying it in her lap for a minute, "I've decided it's come down to this. I can either sit around and remember how my life was till the cows come home and I'm stiff as a poker. But none of that'll ever come back to me.

"So I'm starting out fresh. Today I'm beginning again. What I haven't got, I'll do without and go forward from there."

I chewed my Cherrios, then drank the rest of the milk out of the bowl. Gramma had the right idea. What you don't have, don't worry about. Move on out.

I walked slow back to the kitchen and applied that to me. Okay, I thought, so I was born without certain feelings. I'll just move on ahead without them.

Under my bed, where my empty book was, there lay a little hinged Whitman candy box I had plumb forgot about till I went looking for my book. Inside it were two bottles of perfume. Blue Waltz and Midnight. I opened the Midnight up. It smelled all silver like the moon in the dead of the night. I applied large spills of it to my neck and throat and inside my elbows. Even behind my knees.

If I can't feel anything for a boy, I thought, at least I'll be on the lookout to attract one to me. There wasn't anything written that said they couldn't fall in love with me, never mind how empty I felt about it.

Then I took my book to write in and sat out front on the bridge waiting for Jonah and David to get back from wherever they had gone off to. Jonah had shut his door early and gone on to bed before I saw the face at the back screen, and I wanted to tell him about it. I was sure Mama and Daddy had filled him in, but I was the eyewitness. I wanted to tell him and David myself. And, maybe, while I was reliving the face and my screams and the sheriff coming and Daddy cussing and the sheriff cussing, which I was sure Mama had not told, maybe, while I was recalling all that, maybe David King would smell my Midnight perfume and begin to fall in love with me.

I waited till three forty-five and they didn't put in an appearance. That was long enough to wait for anybody. I had written down two poems and I was tired of *doing*. I felt like just *being* for a while, like taking a walk.

So I tucked the book inside my jeans waistband and headed up the path toward the sawmill. There were several little paths that branched on off of it and I thought I'd follow the first one I came to. I wasn't aiming on actually going to the sawmill. If the Midnight perfume worked like it was supposed to, I sure as heck didn't want Cherokee Fish starting in loving me. The directions said, "Splash on body for allure." It didn't state anything about how to reverse it if it hit the wrong person. I guessed the safest way was to avoid people you didn't plan on wiping out with your allure.

The little path that branched off first took me to the left and well away from the sawmill. I kept climbing, though, and figured I was just heading for the other side of the mountain. This path was overgrown like it wasn't ever traveled much.

Pretty soon I came to another crossroads of paths.

"I better watch myself," I said out loud. "This'll turn out to be like a maze inside a cave. I might never find my way out if I take too many feeder paths."

I kept on a new path I had turned onto. It was about five minutes into it that I heard noise like crashing undergrowth up ahead. I froze right where I was.

Last year Jonah and David King had gone out deer hunting, and, after two and a half hours, Jonah had gone over behind some low bushes to relieve himself. "In the middle of the longest pee in the history of mankind," Jonah had told us that night at supper, "I hear this loud snort and turn around to see the biggest buck I've ever seen in my life. Had to be twelve points. I reckon he thought I was staking out my territory and he was getting ready to claim it back."

I thought of that now and wondered if I could climb a tree fast enough to escape a mad buck when up there in front of me Cherokee Fish busts out of the bushes.

All I could think of was that Midnight perfume I had soaked myself in. But perfume was the last thing on that boy's mind.

"What you doing in the wilderness?" he called. "I thought you stuck to the sawmill."

"I'm just hiking," I hollered back.

He came down the path to where I had stopped in my tracks.

"You always hike with a book in your belt?" he asked, pointing to my empty book.

I pulled it out. It did look pretty dumb, like I was a kangaroo toting her baby.

"I was writing in it and got tired. Didn't have a place to stow it, so I poked it in my waistband."

"Let's see it," he said, grabbing it out of my hands. Suddenly I remembered how quick that boy could turn animal-like.

"Give that back!" I shouted, lunging for it, but he turned and stuck his shoulder between us. "Give me back my book!"

He hadn't opened it yet, thank God. Just stood teasing, his eyes dancing.

"That's private thoughts of mine and I'll thank you to hand it over."

He thought it was funny. He stood right there and laughed with his head thrown back. It made me so mad I slammed him with my fists. When I started that, he dodged around me and took off running down the path I had just hiked up.

I gave chase. There's one thing you can say about me: I don't give up easy. I'm not a quitter. No matter that I might go and get myself killed, I was going to leave this earth with that book in my hand.

Cherokee didn't run so fast I couldn't keep up. I had the feeling he was still toying with me and that, if he'd really wanted to, he could have slid out of sight in no time flat. We reached the sawmill clearing and he leaped atop the sawhorse and walked it like a balance beam. Not even winded.

I lunged at his pants legs to pull him off, but he leaped to the ground before I got hold of them. Then he just stood there grinning, my book behind his back. I was like someone had hold of part of me, had taken it outside my body, and was hanging on to it to tease.

"Say 'Please,'" he said, that half smile right in place. "Then I'll hand you back your private thoughts . . . and lovesick poems."

That made me so mad that, I'm ashamed to say, I busted out crying. Not even Jonah had ever made me this mad.

"Hey," he said, and his eyes suddenly didn't dance anymore. I turned my back to him and scrubbed the tears off my face. I couldn't make up my mind which I hated more, him — or me crying.

"Hey," he said again.

"Hay's for horses," I whipped out and knew I sounded just like my daddy.

"I didn't go to make you *that* mad," he whispered.

"Here's your book, Edie Jo. Must be something powerful special in there to bring out that much fight in you."

I sniffed and turned back around. He handed over the book.

"Just my poems and thoughts," I said, trying to be dignified after blubbering and screaming. I sniffed again. That was taking the place of words. He got the message.

"Had I known it was that special to you, I'd of never snatched it from you. If there's something that private to a person, nobody else has any business messing with it."

I nodded. Looked at the creek. It was like a different person handed me back the book. Different from the one who took it. And I guess if anybody in the world knew about the value of privacy, it would be somebody who lived in a shack down to Davis Bottoms.

I said, "They're pretty personal, my poems and thoughts . . . and then some aren't. I wrote about fog and sunups and all. That ain't personal." I didn't want him to think that book was full of love poems.

"Do you ever let anybody read your poems?" he asked and backed up onto the sawhorse.

"You'd laugh," I said, before he even asked to read them. I looked right straight at him when I said it, too.

But he didn't say, "Who wants to read them?" like Jonah might have. He raised his face a little and looked across at me like I was somebody. Not like I was standing there still sniffing, smelling like a dime-store perfume counter.

"If I give you my word," he said low, and his eyes were serious, no smile, "that I wouldn't laugh? Is that safe enough?"

I thought on it. How'd I know how good that boy's word was? Then I thought, *What's the worst thing that can happen? Say he laughs. Okay. I'll just turn around and walk out of here.* It was worth the risk. And I would have proven to him that girls have thoughts beyond just lovesick poems.

"Okay," I said and sat cross-legged on the ground.

"Read the one about fog. If you've a mind to."

I did. I read it, sitting right there on the ground. It wasn't long.

Fog

*There's something about fog
coming in to the heart of the city
bending to windows
blurring gardens
folding itself between houses
where people keep safe.*

*From what?
Something as gentle as fog?*

E. J. Houp, 1956

I didn't look up at him. Couldn't. It was like admitting to something and not wanting to see the effect. I just sat, picking at the buckle on my sandal. Finally, I said, "I wrote that one morning when we left out of here early and were passing through Asheville on the way to Raleigh."

"I've seen it do that," he said. "Fog."

I looked up. This was not the same Cherokee Fish who grabbed a boy up and like to choked the air out of him. He was just sitting. Calm and peaceful, his eyes so black it hurt to look at them.

"Do you write poems?" I asked. Somebody who had seen inside my poem might write poems himself.

"Nope," he said, leaping down off the sawhorse to dig in his pocket. "Me? I make music."

He flashed his harmonica out and rippled up and down with notes. Quick. Then he grinned like he'd treed a possum. He didn't know I knew that about him. Didn't know I'd already heard his music. And, since he respected privacy, I did, too. I didn't let on it wasn't the first time.

Cherokee Fish played songs I'd never even heard of that day at the sawmill in Half Moon. Elvis Presley and his music couldn't hold a candle to Cherokee Fish. I'd never seen anybody use a harmonica the way he did. The first day I watched him, he must have been practicing, because *this* day he flew along on song after song.

When he stopped, I clapped. It was that good. Normally a person would feel kind of stupid sitting in a clearing, clapping her hands. But his music was that good.

"You could go on television," I told him. "I ain't never heard anybody who could play a harmonica *that* good . . ."

"A what?" he stopped swinging his foot to ask.

"A harmonica," I said.

"A mouth organ," he corrected me.

"A mouth organ?" I was beginning to feel like Mary Grady.

He grinned. "Now it's a cigar and I'm Groucho Marx." He held the mouth organ like a fat cigar and tapped it with his back two fingers to unload the ashes.

I just sat and watched him. He wasn't any Cherokee Fish I knew. He was like anybody else. And he had kept his word, not laughing at my poem. That was pushing it for a boy to not laugh at poems. Jonah would have. And Jonah didn't always keep his word. He most always bent things around to his way. Not Cherokee, I guessed.

"Look, if I'm boring you, I can leave now," he said, holding the mouth organ up like he was fixing to take a puff off it.

"No. No," I said. "Do some more."

He shook his head and hopped down. "That's the way Groucho Marx talks. I saw him on the television downtown in the show window of Slathern's Furniture Company."

"Where'd you learn to play like that?" I asked him from where I sat.

He stretched and stuffed the mouth organ down into his jeans pocket before he answered. "My grandaddy taught me. From before I can recollect I've been playing. Just learned it from him and picked out songs for myself."

"Yeah, but you play like a pro. People would pay money to hear somebody play like you do."

He didn't even answer. Just grinned and walked toward the creek. "Playing that long makes me thirsty," he said, and, leaning down, he cupped water with his hand and slurped it.

Then he sat back on his heels and looked across at me. "Do you know why I just don't lean on over and drink right out of the creek?"

I shook my head no.

"Because, in the old days, a Indian didn't never let hisself get in a position to be off balance lest a animal or another human being jump him." He wiped his mouth on his arm.

"What part Indian are you?" I asked, innocent as Mary, Jesus' mother. I was looking for him to answer that on his daddy's side he was full-blooded Cherokee. Or something like that. It never occurred to me he'd take offense at the question. But he looked across at me in a new way, like I was a stranger . . . like I was that human being fixing to jump him. "I didn't mean nothing wrong by asking that," I said.

His eyes moved on down to the ground and he squinted like he was seeing something beyond where we were. Maybe he was looking back at his past, because he finally said, "Half Cherokee, half white. I'm a half-breed."

As God in heaven is my witness, I hadn't heard the sadness that heavy in anybody's voice ever before. Not even Gramma's that day I came upon her.

"Cherokee," I said. That was the first time I'd ever called him by his name. "That ain't nothing to fret about, you being a half-breed. I'm half this and half . . ."

Boy! His eyes slashed back up to me faster than a lightning strike.

"I don't like nobody else to call me that," he whispered. "As far as I'm concerned, I'm Indian and proud of it."

"I'm sorry," I whispered back, remembering he hadn't been this kind to Skeeter Runyon.

Then I told him what my Gramma had said that morning about going forward, careful never to mention the word *arson*. It wasn't just to fill up the quiet that had settled in. I thought it might help him find his way through being a half-breed, but I was careful not to say that, either.

"This ain't no sermon," I said when I'd wound down. "I know you don't like sermons. I just figured it might help to hear how somebody else is dealing with their troubles."

He had sat off his heels on down on the ground while

I talked, his arms resting on his knees. When I finished, he just sat like that, watching nothing in specific. Just watching. I wondered did he hear one word.

Finally he got up and went over for more water.

"How can you drink that stuff?" I said.

He looked over his shoulder at me from where he squatted and grinned. "It's good. Try some."

"Yuck! Not with all them crayfish and polliwogs stirring around in it. No way, Hosea! Not me."

"It comes from a spring right up the mountain a ways, Edie Jo."

When I looked like I didn't believe a word, he spread his hands. "Honest. No lie."

I shook my head. "There ain't enough thirst inside me to *ever* drink that nasty stuff. Jonah says there's water moccasins all in the creek, and I've seen 'em myself out on the bridge, sunning. Snake water!"

"What's wrong with you, Miss Houp?" he called, standing up, a laugh coming back into his voice. "You afraid of something as gentle as spring water?"

He froze the way he stood just long enough for me to know he was making reference to my poem about people keeping safe from something as gentle as fog. So he did hear, just didn't all the time feel the need to let on he heard. Then he leaned over and cupped his hands and tried to splash that cold water all the way over to where I sat.

"You can't reach me," I called.

And he couldn't. But almost.

10

My mama has a kindness in her, down deep. I've seen, this is the truth, I've seen her chase a lady walking out of the women's restroom at the S & W Cafeteria in Asheville, trying to step on a strip of toilet paper stuck to the heel of the lady's shoe. Now, you've really got to care about people to put yourself in that position and the person you've helped never even be aware of it.

But when she's crossed, she can be mean as a diamondback rattler looking for food. Daddy crossed her back in the spring, and even when it was the middle of June she was mad as she'd been to start with. It wasn't letting up any. I reckoned Gramma was beginning to believe that was the way Mama and Daddy had lived twenty years of marriage.

Mama was so mad, she'd even been forgetting to stew up prunes with lemon slices to set in the middle of the kitchen table. Either she forgot, or she didn't care whether we were reg'lar or not.

That night at supper, Mama's anger seeped on out some more because of something that happened, and, for the first time since the feud began, Daddy set her straight.

I had come on back from the sawmill along about quarter to six and shoved my empty book under the cot and wandered on back to the kitchen.

"Where you been, Edie Jo?" Mama snapped, which should have been a warning flag right there. Normally she doesn't care that I go off for a walk, long as I'm back in time to set the table.

"For a walk," I said, lathering the bar of Ivory soap on my hands till they were white.

"I think it's time you started taking an interest in cooking," she said. I wondered if the thought had just occurred to her. She hadn't ever mentioned it before.

"I'm here now," I told her, wiping my hands on a paper towel.

"Don't get smart with me."

The feeling that had begun to grow inside of me when I had listened to Cherokee's music and when he had listened to my poem — a feeling of peace and . . . *happiness* isn't enough . . . a beginning of joy, maybe — that feeling blew away like fog in a wind. I just looked at her.

"Set the table," she said and kept on cooking.

We were about halfway through supper when the doorbell rang.

"Edie Jo, get that," Mama snapped again.

When I opened the front door, Sheriff Stringfield was

standing out there. I turned on the yellow front-porch light and asked him on in.

"I hate to disturb your family at dinnertime, little lady," he said to me. "But I need to talk to your daddy."

"I'll go get him," I said and got as far as the door to the hall before I remembered my manners. "Have a seat," I said, turning back to say it.

Not only Daddy but all of us came out and stood there waiting to see what the sheriff had come to tell Daddy.

"Horace," he began. I wondered was he still mad at my daddy or did men fire up and then just get over it fast. "Our boys found something of interest this afternoon that may be what we've been waiting for."

"Here, Ottis, have a seat there," Daddy said, maybe anticipating it was going to take a while. We all sat. "Now, go on."

"Harry Purvis and Jim Woolard went back to your mama's empty lot." He stopped to glance at Gramma. "They were going to comb the area one more time.

"You know that little drainage ditch that cuts across the back of the property?" he asked and Gramma nodded. "Well, there's a clump of bushes down there —"

"Hydrangeas. I planted them myself," she butted in to say.

"Well, Harry was groping around under one of them bushes, and felt something that moved when his hands fell on it. He tugged it out of there and it was the beat-uppest windbreaker you ever seen."

"Windbreaker?" I said.

"It's a jacket, Hot Shot," Jonah said. But our eyes didn't leave the sheriff.

"Inside the right-hand pocket there was, along with a empty pack of Marlboros, a parking ticket dated April 13, two days before the fire. So that jacket was stuffed under there after April 13."

"Well, can you trace the parking ticket by the number or something? The license plate?" Mama hopped in to ask.

"Yes ma'am, we can," he said. He had laid his hat on the arm of the chair where he was sitting, and it fell off onto the floor. I scooped it up and handed it to him. "Thank you, little lady. We've done just that this afternoon, Miz Houp." He looked over at Mama. "The car belongs to one Sierra Fish. It's a 'forty-nine Plymouth, black coupe."

I didn't hear the next things he told. I was too busy thinking about Sierra Fish. *Fish,* I thought. *Can't be too many families named that. Wonder if Cherokee knows this Sierra Fish?*

"Well," the sheriff stood to go and I tuned back in, "I knew you'd want to know. Like I say, the family lives down to Davis Bottoms. We're keeping this strictly confidential until we can do some more investigating and see what we can come up with.

"It don't necessarily mean this person is suspect. This

is what you call circumstantial evidence. He could claim somebody stuck that windbreaker under that bush last week, and he might be telling the truth. On the other hand," he nodded, "it might be just what we need.

"I understand this Fish guy's got a couple of brothers and several sisters. We got to string out our net careful so's we catch the right person."

Family? Davis Bottoms? I wished I hadn't tuned out and missed what all he said.

When the sheriff left, that's when Mama hit rock bottom.

"See there," she hissed before the sheriff had even driven out of the yard. "A bunch of half-breeds done it. And here you want to go and integrate with them people." She glared at my daddy, her lips tight.

Why, I don't know, but that picture of Mama and Daddy on their wedding day filtered across my mind. The picture that used to hang in Gramma's house and got burned up in the fire. *How do people change,* I thought, *from looking at each other like they can't wait to be alone to this . . . to where they'd be afraid to be alone with each other?*

"Don't start in, Helen," Daddy said, heading toward what was left of his cold supper in the kitchen.

"That's right!" she says. "Leave. That's so characteristic of you, Horace. Turn tail and run, once things heat up. You stirred up the sediment of integration, but when the water gets cloudy, where are you? I don't see you palling around with them. I don't hear you —"

· 97 ·

Daddy, swift like an animal that's taken more than it ever intended, turned and covered the space between him and Mama in two strides of his long legs.

"Don't," he shouted, "ever bring this up again!" Each word was a bullet he shot toward her. "Look what you're teaching your children, Helen. 'Because your skin is dark and you are down on your luck, I know what that means. Without a doubt. It means you are lazy and stupid and a worthless person. So, quick! before you get away, let me stomp on you like a cockroach. Let me squash the life right out of you!'"

Mama's jaw hung slack. But Daddy wasn't through. Not by a long shot.

"Those people are human beings with dreams same as we've got. You talk about adding on a room to this house someday? Do you think they don't dream, too? When a mother down to Davis Bottoms watches her children going out the door to school, don't you reckon she feels the same pride we do?

"And where the hell do you come off thinking we, of *all* people, are better? My God!"

He turned away from her. "We live in a little-bitty house, in a little dirt-scratched yard, on the outskirts of small-town America."

He just stood looking at the floor, his hands jammed in his pockets.

Finally, Mama gathered up the front of her apron like it was part of her body she was keeping from flying loose and walked on past Daddy out toward the kitchen.

11

When Mary Grady rang me up on the telephone later that evening and asked could I spend Tuesday night with her, I would have gone even if Mama had said no. I needed to get to someplace where war wasn't brewing, bad.

We had this game we played, Mary Grady and me. She lived in a neighborhood with a street and sidewalks and a park a block over. Not in a holler in a mountain like me. After dark, whenever I spent the night with her in warm weather, we would go out spying on people. It was like we were FBI agents and we reported to J. Edgar Hoover over make-believe walkie-talkies.

The best part was the park, though once we watched a man in the shower at his house. We couldn't help he didn't have enough sense to pull the window shade. You couldn't see below his waist anyhow. But the park was the perfect place for the game. We'd dart behind bushes and trees. Sometimes there'd be couples making out on the benches. Tonight there were a few.

"Why do they call it 'making out'?" Mary Grady

asked as we stood against a brick wall and peeped around it at one couple going to town. "Kissing and all."

"I don't know," I whispered back, "but he'd better let her go so she can breathe."

Mary Grady giggled.

"Shut up," I whispered. "You want them to hear us?"

She couldn't quit. It was funny. It was like they were glued together with household cement. Then, as if the giggling wasn't enough, Mary Grady started in coughing. That they heard. The boy pulled away and looked around while the girl fluffed out her long hair. When he turned to look around, his face suddenly caught the streetlight and I sucked in air to my socks.

"Jonah," I whispered to Mary Grady. "And that must be Emily."

Talk about a sobering thought. It wasn't funny anymore. I just wanted to get out of there with my life. Jonah took after Daddy in his temper.

As soon as he looked the other way, I slipped into the shadows, Mary Grady right behind.

Now that I knew Emily and Jonah were that serious, it made me feel all the more like part of me was missing. Here I was, thirteen years old, and had never even kissed a boy. Not even held hands. That night at Mary Grady's, I dreamed about it. In my dream, we were at a picture show with Dale Robertson starring in it. All of a sudden, he walked right off the screen, on down into the audience, stopped at our row, took my hand, and led me out of that theater on outside till we found the park. And there on a park bench, like Jonah and Emily, he kissed me. When I woke up from the dream, it was so real I felt like I *had* been kissed.

When I got home from Mary Grady's, I did what chores Mama had written on the side of the Frigidaire for me to do. She didn't use paper to make a chore list. Wrote right on the Frigidaire with a pencil and scrubbed the chores off when they were done. Today it was "Wipe down the front-porch furniture with a cloth and a basin of soapy water, then wet-mop the whole tile porch." It didn't take long. Then I was free to go until time to set the table for supper.

"Edie Jo," Mama called from the kitchen, talking over top of Paul Harvey's news for the day on the radio, "you remember you asked me to get some books for you at the library next time I drove into Asheville? Well, there's two books on my bed I checked out for you at the library yesterday."

"All right," I called from the hall. I cut into Mama's room. One book was *The Secret Garden*. That was possible. Garden? Naw. Secret? Maybe. The other one was *The Yearling*. *The Yearling!* That was the book my teacher, Mrs. Johnson, read to us this year, for thirty minutes after lunch every day. I loved that book.

"Now," I said, scooping it up and leaving, "I can read it for myself."

I carried it with me and settled on the swing. I would have gone all the way to the sawmill because it was private there, except when Cherokee showed up, but it was too early. I'd have to wait until the four o'clock whistle from town for the sawmill to empty of people.

The book moved slow, but as I read I could hear Mrs. Johnson in my mind — her big, hollow voice reading it. She may have had to sit on us during math every day, but during the time she read that book to us, not a person budged. At the end of the book, the boy behind me, James Earl, he put his head down on his desk and bawled like a baby. At the rate I was going, I knew it'd be at least a week before I got to that part.

When the four o'clock blew, I folded down the corner of the page and headed on out for the sawmill, carrying the book. I believe I was half wishing Cherokee Fish would show up. I thought maybe I could get him to talk about his family and the name Sierra Fish might come up. Anyway, he made life interesting. His music was enough to draw a person back to hear more. But if he didn't come, I could read along in the book.

I had just gotten comfortable over by the ledge when, sure enough, I heard that boy whistling. I looked up in time to see him bust out of the woods.

"What you up to, Cherokee Fish?" I hollered. I didn't want to catch him off guard. Wanted him to know I was there from the get-go.

He stopped and looked across the creek at me. Smiled a little more than his usual smile. I could tell he was glad I was there.

"You writing in a different book, aren't you?" he called, motioning at my book.

"No, no," I said, laughing. "I'm reading this one, not writing it." I got up and crossed the creek without falling on my butt.

"Hey! You're getting good at that," he said. Then he just smiled and stood.

"What're you grinning at, boy?" I asked and sat cross-legged on the pine needles.

"I'm grinning," he said, squatting down in front of me, "because I brought you something." He held his closed fists out. "Pick," he says.

I tapped his left hand. He opened it empty. "Missed," he said. So I tapped his right hand. He opened it empty, too. "Missed again," he said.

Jonah did this to me twice a month at least. I was used to it. "Must be a boy's game," I said, looking him cold right in the eye. "My brother does this on a regular basis, among other things."

"Other things?" he said, rolling back to sit on the ground.

"Yeah. He used to hold weekly lessons on being scared of the dark, for one thing."

"And you believed him?" he asked. "You're scared of the dark?" He laughed.

"You bet," I said, feeling my Daddy's nature rise in me. "He's a good teacher."

"Well," he said, propping his arms on his bent-up knees, "you think you could unlearn it, being afraid of the dark?"

"I doubt it."

He looked over at the creek and nodded slow.

"You're probably right," he said, still looking. "You can't learn what you don't want to learn."

I watched him. Wondered why he'd told me he had something for me when he didn't.

"You know," he looked back to me, "I used to be afraid of the dark." He nodded. "I did."

"How come you to get rid of it?"

"Well," he drew a deep breath like it was going to be a long story, "I found the dark could be useful."

"Useful?" I asked, and suddenly I saw in my mind people moving in the dark, setting my gramma's house afire. I fought seeing that. Frowned.

"You can be in the dark and be private," he said. "When you live as close as I do, so many people crammed in together, you take privacy any way you can get it.

"The dark is . . . friendly. It's quiet. It's safe."

These were not things I found in the dark, except in my corner of the living room. We were so far apart, I couldn't think of anything to say.

Finally, he pointed at my book and asked, "What's your book about?"

Good Lord. I didn't mean to tell him the whole story. I just started out and told the beginning. He rolled back and lay down, listening. Rested his head on his hands. Every time I come to a stopping place, he said, "And then what?" So it came down to the end, and I near cried remembering James Earl bawling like he did.

Cherokee sat up. "That's one sad story," he said, shaking his head. "You gonna write stories like that? About the mountains of North Carolina, about these mountains?"

I nodded. "About this sawmill," I said. "This here is my favorite place in Half Moon."

"Mine, too." He reached into his jeans pocket for something. Couldn't dig it out, so he stood up to get to it. "I really did bring you something," he told me.

I perked up. I should have known. He'd kept his word before. He wouldn't have said it if it weren't true.

He squatted back down and held his hand opened flat out. "This here is a arrowhead," he said.

I picked it up. It was warm from his body. It looked blunt, but when I ran my finger across the edge, it was sharp. Somebody had worked on that edge. It definitely had an arrowhead shape to it.

"I don't know how old it is, but it's real," he told me. "It was a arrowhead made by some American Indian somewhere, sometime . . . a long time ago."

I just blew out air. Picturing this little stone being shaped by someone maybe a hundred or more years ago made me feel outside myself. I could feel the woods alive with Indians the way it was, see them moving along the creek, silent as part of the woods themselves.

I looked over at Cherokee, knew I was looking at the great-great-grandson of one of those long-ago Indians.

"You like it?" he asked, looking at me straight.

"Yes," I whispered. "You sure you want me to have it?"

He nodded. "Yeah. My brother gave it to me a long time ago."

"Your brother?" Something deep inside me, narrow as a thread, began tightening, tensing up, waiting for an answer I thought I might not want to be hearing.

"Yeah. I got two brothers. One, Emanuel. He moved west when I was eleven. He's the one that gave me the arrowhead. The only brother left at home is Sierra. He's twenty-one. Then I got sisters, too. Three of them."

I know we must have talked, but all I could hang on to was that Sierra was his brother, lived in his house. The sheriff had said he wanted to spread the net carefully so they'd catch the right person. I didn't want to but I couldn't help myself — I wondered if it could have been Cherokee moving quick in the night to set my gramma's house afire.

Cherokee was saying something to me about me writing a poem about the nighttime. What he didn't realize was that suddenly I was there. In the nighttime. Inside my head. It was private, all right. But it wasn't safe. It wasn't friendly. It was just quiet and very frightening. As cold as that arrowhead sitting on my windowsill later. Cold and hard and real.

12

Even when I woke up the next morning and nighttime was well gone, the blackness in my mind pushed itself tight. I lay there in my cot with my eyes closed against daylight, trying to figure out how Cherokee was innocent and how Sierra Fish set the fire all by his lonesome. And why.

I did write the poem about nighttime that morning, to free up my mind and keep me from dwelling on the arson thing. That afternoon I went to the sawmill on the chance Cherokee might show up and I could read it to him. I waited until it was near dark. I had given up on him and was gathering up, getting ready to leave, when I heard a whistle from the edge of the woods. I looked up quick to see if it was him. It was.

"You by yourself?" he called, but soft. He was standing there with his thumbs hooked in his jeans belt loops.

"Sure," I said, coming his way across the creek. "Why?"

"I didn't know but what you brought the sheriff with you. His men been to my house asking questions. About arson."

I just looked level at him. He hadn't asked the first question of me, and I wasn't putting forth more than was called for.

"Well," he said, dropping to the pine straw, "I know it wasn't me that did any arson. That's what I know and what I told the sheriff's men."

I just watched him, wanted to believe, but when his eyes found their way to mine, I dropped my gaze to the book in my hand.

"You brought your book," he pointed out.

"Yeah," I said, sitting down.

"D'you write that poem on night yet?"

I nodded, quick. It was hard to share what I put down on paper. Even with Cherokee. I wasn't like Cherokee, where the music just flowed natural from him. I didn't give up my writing easy.

"Let's hear it," he said and lay back on the ground.

I opened the book to the poem. The words were there, but my voice couldn't say them. How could I read my thoughts to him when I couldn't be honest and tell him what I knew about the arson investigation? I just stared at the page.

Finally he sat up and said, soft-like, "Give me the book. I'll read it."

He took the book, but before he turned it toward him to read, he said, "It's okay, Edie Jo." I didn't know what all he meant. It's okay that I don't share my words as easy as he does his music or it's okay about the arson thing, that he knew I was holding back on him and knew I'd be hearing soon enough what I didn't want to hear about the fire setting. About Sierra. I didn't ask, though. I just looked into his dark eyes.

"You know," he says, turning the book around toward him, "you're gonna have to learn to read what you write out loud to people. A poem isn't a poem till it's read out loud, no more than a song is till it's sung."

He sat cross-legged and propped the book across his knees. "I don't read perfect," he told me without looking up. "Just so you know."

Then he read.

Night

God drops his jacks
on a velvet cloth.
He ponders.
Then,
bouncing the ball,
he gathers them
one
by
one.

E. J. Houp, 1956

He looked up, not even the half smile there. "How'd you do that? Write and compare?"

"The way you make music," I said.

He grinned, leaned way back to pull out the mouth

organ, and sat back up to say, "A little music to match your poem about night."

Then he played something quiet and sad, lonesome as night itself. When he was done he smiled and signed his name, the way I had signed mine. "C. Fish, 1956," he said.

I held out my hand for my book but he put his hand there instead. In a handshake. "Nice meeting you, E. J. Houp." Then he stood up, and when he leaned down to hand me the book, I felt him touch my hair with his hand.

"I'd say your hair might be shiny as a star," he said. Then leaping back, he spread his hands and shouted, "Hey! Is that a poem or what?" Froze in that position like a spell had been cast.

To unfreeze him, I knew I had to answer. "It's a poem. Now you're a poet *and* a musician. How's that for talent!"

He whirled in a tight circle, and when he came to a stop, he stomped his foot once. Hard.

"Ever seen a war dance?" he asked, his eyes full of fun.

I shook my head. "Was that it?"

"Nope. That was a peace dance. The shortened version. I'd stay and do the whole thing for you, but night's coming on and you might get scared."

That's when I looked around and saw how dark had begun to fall without me seeing it. I hadn't even noticed.

"Aha!" he said, pointing a finger. "You see. It's not

the dark you're afraid of. It's a habit you teach yourself every day."

I hated the way he turned his head to one side and watched me like he was the teacher of the world. Smiling.

I just stood.

"Well, just so there's no panic, I'll walk you to your clearing," he said.

That night I dreamed Cherokee Fish kissed me, on the mouth, tender. He leaned over top of me where I lay on the pine straw at the sawmill and kissed me, letting his body down slow till it weighed heavy on mine. The kiss lasted a long time. When I woke up, I knew I hadn't been born missing. That feeling wasn't meant for David King, so it hadn't come. I began to understand that it was meant for Cherokee Fish.

And, even though there was a whole part of me knowing that to be in love with an Indian boy would be beyond disaster, that not only my family but every single person in Half Moon would hate me and feed their hatred every morning of their lives, the feeling was still here. I just shut all those doors in my mind and lived in the rooms full of sunshine, full of Cherokee Fish.

That next day I went around with a wholeness, a feeling deep and good. Oh, there were voices that whispered inside. *What would your mama say? And Jonah? Those half-breeds nearly killed you and Jonah that time.*

I just ignored the voices. Clamped them shut and let the wholeness soak in.

That feeling stayed till late afternoon, even if it was storming outside. As it turned out, I didn't once think of arson. The rain couldn't even reach where I was.

The doorbell rang along about five-thirty. It was the sheriff. We sat in the living room like we'd done before, Daddy asking the questions, the rest of us quiet.

"Well," Sheriff Stringfield said, "here's where we stand. We've questioned friends and neighbors of the Fish boy and we've even questioned him and his family."

"Yes?" Daddy said, leaning forward to catch every word the sheriff threw out. Me? I was wanting to back up to the hall door and on down the hall through the dining room and the kitchen and on out into the back yard. I wondered if Sierra Fish had been the face at the back porch that night. Or Cherokee? Not Cherokee, I thought. He couldn't have given me an arrowhead and it be him. One thing about Cherokee Fish: if he hated, he hated. There wasn't any pretending in that boy.

"The mother," Sheriff Stringfield said and I tried to picture Cherokee's mother in my mind, "she doesn't recall where Sierra was on the night in question, which is normal. I'd suspect something if she did remember that far back. But she did say she doesn't think her son has any animosity toward you, Miz Houp." He nodded to Gramma. "Or toward the Truitts."

"She would say that," Daddy said, "if she has any realization of why you are questioning her."

The sheriff nodded. "Right. Sierra Fish doesn't remember his whereabouts on the night of April fifteenth neither. We're in the process of getting us a search warrant, at this point, because I have a feeling we might find some incriminating evidence on the premises. This guy is no hardened criminal. If he did it, he's made a mistake along the way. I guarantee it. I'll let you know, in the next day or so, what we find."

"Please do," Daddy said.

The sheriff turned toward Gramma. "Miz Houp, I want you to continue to search your memory for any contact you may have had with this Fish boy. Even though it may seem inconsequential to you. Any contact with any Indians at all."

"Well, you know . . ." Gramma stopped to clear her throat. "There comes to mind, and I had clean forgot it till now, but somebody rung my doorbell and asked for work back in early April. If I remember correctly, he offered to clean the gutters and scrape and paint the garage." She stopped and thought.

"You can't remember what he looked like?" the sheriff asked her, pulling a little spiral tablet out from his shirt pocket.

Gramma sat, trying. She started to say something once, then stopped.

"Any kind of description of him and what took place would be helpful," the sheriff said.

"Well, I do, a little," Gramma said. "I do remember because he was so tall he plumb filled the door frame.

When I told him I didn't need help, I was counting on my grandson pitching in, he said he needed the money bad. That's when I reached up and locked the screen door, scared he might try to force his way in.

"But he left. We didn't pass words, angry words. He cut across the yard and I called out to him, 'I wish you people would learn to use a sidewalk.' He stopped, but he never even turned around. After a minute or so he walked on off. He didn't use the sidewalk, though."

"Was he Indian?" the sheriff asked.

She nodded. "I believe so."

We waited for her to remember more. But there wasn't any more. That was all there was. Not enough to make a person go to the trouble of setting a house afire. Not unless they were crazy or pushed into the last corner.

"Well," the sheriff stood, "I thank you, ma'am. You never can tell if that will be helpful or not. If I can, I'll try to get a photograph of this Fish boy and see can you recollect if he was the one. And his brother, too," the sheriff said and left.

I locked the front-door screen behind him and turned on the yellow porch light. It wasn't even starting in dark yet, but I needed it somehow, to keep the dark from coming.

13

Ever since Mama and Daddy boiled over at each other, there began a softness coming round in Mama. Her eyes somehow weren't quite as cold, and she smiled now and then. I couldn't figure it out. It might have been just that the clearing of the air had relieved tension. I wondered, too, did it have anything to do with folks forgetting my daddy's stand on integration. I wondered if they were speaking again to Mama. At church, people were beginning to be friendly again, for the most part. Except old Mrs. Hensinger. I didn't reckon she'd ever speak to us again, and I didn't much care. At least it'd spare us from hearing her "don't you know" at the end of everything she said.

July Fourth, we went to the fireworks in Asheville because they were bigger than what Half Moon could come up with. That's what Mama said.

The next Sunday, after dinner, the phone rang. It was Mary Grady for me. She wanted me to spend the night with her because Monday was her birthday.

"Let me call you back," I told her. "I gotta find Mama to ask her."

"No. Don't. The people on the party line hog the phone. You might never get me. I'll just hang on. Take your time."

Mama was lying down on her bed, reading the Sunday *Asheville Citizen.*

"Mary Grady's birthday is tomorrow," I started out, fully expecting a great big *no* since it hadn't been a week that I'd spent the night over to her house. "And she's asked me to spend the night to celebrate." I braced myself.

Mama put the paper down and looked at me. "Don't be staying all day tomorrow, 'cause you've got chores to do," she said. "I'll run you over there when I'm done with the paper."

As easy as that. Maybe Mama's mad had finally peaked and the days of feuding would be behind us.

I hit Mary Grady's about four o'clock. I put my overnight case and pillow into her room. Then we went for a walk.

"Not to the park," I told her. "I don't want no part of that ever again."

I showed her a dirt road near her house that I'd seen before. It had a metal chain across it with a lock, like it was a driveway not in use anymore. Jonah had told me he camped out once up that road a ways.

"Let's see where it goes," she said.

Nothing like a chain and a padlock to make you want to go on the other side of them and find out what's important enough to keep you out. The road was overgrown and sloped gentle up.

"Ain't been used in a long time," I said.

She nodded. Thank God she was moving beyond that echo stuff she used to do.

The road ended after a while at the foot of a rise. Big deal. Nothing worth locking up after all. There was a path leading up.

"You wanna try it?" I asked her. She shrugged. "'S *your* birthday," I told her. She nodded.

It was steep going. We grabbed hold of saplings and roots to pull ourselves along.

"Whew, Law!" I gasped, knowing for the first time what Gramma meant when she said it.

We sat to rest on a rock and then followed the narrow path on down and then up again.

"We'd better blaze a trail," I turned around to say. Mary Grady looked puzzled. "Leave markings to find our way back," I explained.

She nodded, but we didn't do it.

When we reached the top of a little mountain, we sat again to rest. A creek was running by the trail and I squatted down to splash water on my face, remembering how Cherokee said an Indian never used to let himself get into a position he couldn't protect himself from. I even tasted the water and it wasn't bad.

"What time you got?" I asked her.

"Ten of five," she said. "Let's keep on. We're this far. I want to see where it goes."

We had started down the other side of the mountain on a narrow little trail, single file, when we began to hear voices calling to each other.

"Sure does echo on a mountain, don't it?" Mary Grady commented.

"Yeah," I answered her, but stopped walking because there was a certain tone to the voices that shouted back and forth. "Do they sound mad?" I turned to ask Mary Grady.

"Maybe," she said, listening.

We walked on down the path. The closer we came to the voices, the madder they sounded. There were cuss words sailing around like gnats in a swarm.

"You're lying, goddamn it!" this one voice screamed. "I *know* you told!"

"I'm *not* lying. *You're* the liar!" another voice shot back. "You followed me up here just to accuse me, you son of a bitch!"

I turned and looked at Mary Grady. "They're mad," I said. "*Real* mad. I think maybe we'd better be getting on back. It's near suppertime and nightfall."

"*Aw-w-w,*" she whined, "what would it hurt to listen?" But I pushed her gentle on back the way we came.

We had gone about ten yards when one word spilled itself out of a string of words being yelled and broadsided me. "You do what you have to do," this one voice hollered. "But I am *not* taking the blame for arson. I didn't do it and I'm not taking the blame."

Arson. I yanked Mary Grady's shirt. "Stop," I whispered, hoarse. "We got to go back, get closer."

"Why?" she asked.

But I had already turned and was walking slow and

careful back toward the voices. When I could see people yelling through the trees, about half a football field away, I looked for a place to stop and watch from — but hidden, so they couldn't see us. We came to a crop of low fir trees and I slid off the path and in behind them.

"Why'd you change your mind?" Mary Grady slid in behind me and asked.

"I want to see who's talking about arson, that's why."

We could stand right there and halfway see three figures in a clearing of some sort. They were still hollering so loud I figured they'd not hear us if we downshifted toward them, real slow-like. I wanted to find out who would be yelling about arson. We moved when they shouted, and stopped in the silences.

Suddenly, we came upon just the right spot for watching. It was behind some mountain laurel, thick with leaves. We just held some branches down and could see through the opening, perfect.

The first thing my eyes found was the sawmill. About twenty-five feet up ahead. The sawmill? Good grief! We must have walked five miles, I thought, to get from Mary Grady's house back to the sawmill. But there were the buildings grouped over against the side of the mountain, the pile of sawdust making a yellow hill off to the side.

That was my creek, then, I thought. I remembered Cherokee had told me it came from a spring farther up the mountain.

The next thing I recognized was one of the three people. My mouth must have flopped open a foot.

"That there's Cherokee Fish," Mary Grady poked me to whisper.

I nodded. It was true. And he was doing his share of the cussing along with the other two. One of them was sort of short. The third was tall and thin and had his back to us so I couldn't see much of him. I could hear him, though. Shouting.

"How else did the sheriff know to look in that chicken house?" he asked Cherokee. "Me and Arlie had covered everything with dead leaves and nobody would of even thought to look out there if you hadn't pointed him in that direction —"

"How'd I know?" Cherokee came back at him fast. "How'd I know you and Arlie was stupid enough to leave your damn incriminating evidence out for everybody to see? The sheriff asked me where our property ended and I showed him."

The tall boy reached one long arm out and tried to pick Cherokee up by the neck of his T-shirt, but Cherokee broke his hold with a chop of his arm. He might have been shorter, but I figured he was powerful enough to take care of himself.

"Just tell me one thing," Cherokee shouted in the tall one's face. "Why the hell did you want to go around starting fires? Did you have a reason of some sort?"

"Yes, I had a reason," the tall one answered back, and the one he had called Arlie nodded. "I was sick and tired of being called 'you people' like we're some mangy breed of animal. I hear it everywhere I go. That old lady, she called me that — 'you people.' She —"

"You set her house afire because she called you 'you people'?" Cherokee asked, not believing.

The tall one jabbed his finger at Cherokee and shouted, "Listen, man, that ain't all she done. She reached up and locked the screen door like she was afraid she might have to get close enough to breathe my air. People been locking doors on me all my life. Well, I am damn sure tired of it. A person can take only so much rejection, then he snaps. I'm a human being, not a animal. I want —"

"And you set her house on fire because she locked her door?"

"You damn straight," the tall one said.

I knew the 'old lady' was Gramma. It was the same story she had told the sheriff.

"I'm half-breed, too, Sierra," Cherokee said, then turned and walked away. "I don't go around setting fires and murdering . . ."

So this was Sierra. *Sweet Jesus, I do pray,* I thought, *what have we stumbled on?* I began to understand that me and Mary Grady wouldn't have a chance if we were found. We'd be as good as dead. I wasn't sure even Cherokee could protect us. Maybe he wouldn't want to. They were thrashing this arson thing out between them, and it was meant for no other ears.

"Mary Grady," I whispered low. She turned and

looked at me. "This is serious, and me and you, we're in danger for our lives if they see or hear us."

I reckon my eyes were solemn enough, maybe so scared, that she understood. She nodded and looked back through her peephole. This wasn't any spy game on Jonah making out with Emily. This was a deadly game, and we were trapped till somebody broke.

It's funny how the smells of the woods in the mountains can be a comfort to a person. It's not a particular smell, like one flower; it's the greenness of pine needles and the sweet odor wet wood gives off that soothes a person. Usually. I could smell the woods while I stood with Mary Grady that afternoon, but the smell just reminded me how trapped we were. Afraid to retreat now that we knew what kind of battle was going on at the sawmill. We had positioned ourselves too close before we found out, and now, by instinct, we knew our safety lay in freezing as still and silent as trees.

Cherokee turned back to Sierra. "And so," Cherokee asked, "what'd old man Truitt do to you? Lock his screen door and call you 'you people'?"

"Son of a bitch!" Sierra hissed.

"Sierra, listen." Cherokee's voice came to a normal level. "Man, this isn't the way. You can't go round burning people out just because they piss you off. You —"

"Take it then. Eat it up. But I'm not. Not anymore. I'm done with taking it. You do it your way. I'll do it mine," Sierra said and turned toward where we stood, hidden, twenty feet away. In the moment I saw his face, I knew I had seen him before. This was the face that had pushed itself into my car window that night Jonah and I nearly got ourselves killed. And those hands had rubbed my hair. I had forgotten until this moment how terrified I'd been. And, in the remembering, the terror came back. My mouth opened for air, but none was coming in. There wasn't any space in my lungs for it. My chest was tight. Squeezed. I knew I had to get out of there.

I had just turned to leave, to chance it, when Cherokee fired off a volley at Sierra that turned the whole fight inside out. "Say what you want to," Cherokee said, and his voice was set and determined. It was the voice he had used that day in square-dancing class, while we all watched, standing under the torn basketball hoop. "You're not pulling me into this. I'll tell the sheriff that I don't know nothing about it, and that's what I'll do to help you. I don't know nothing about it *unless* he tells me I did it. You need to know right now that I'm not taking any blame for your arson."

Sierra wheeled around and Cherokee pointed his finger right at him. "'Cause if they start pulling me into it, I'm not afraid to tell them," Cherokee said. "I'll flat out tell what I think happened. That you and Arlie got you some fire starters tied together out there in that shack Ma used to raise chickens in. I don't know just how you did it. I wasn't there, so I can only guess. But I do know nobody's gon' blame me for it." He nodded his head and finished, "I'll tell you that this one last time." Cherokee's smile was back, stubborn, daring Sierra.

They glared at each other like two tomcats, squaring off to fight. But Cherokee must have said all he was going to say, because he turned toward the path to leave. Suddenly Sierra sprang like an animal, straight at Cherokee's back. He hammered his fist into the back of Cherokee's head so strong that Cherokee crumpled where he had stood and sprawled on the ground.

"You're right about that!" Sierra yelled down at him. "You've said it for the last time!"

He and Arlie stood and watched Cherokee, waiting for him to come round. But he just lay there at Sierra's feet. Finally, Sierra nudged him with the toe of his shoe. "Wake up, little brother," he sneered, soft-like. "Nap time's over."

That was when his voice reached my memory and I recollected how his voice could be. A little high. There's a word, *sinister,* and that tells his voice.

Arlie laughed and came close to stand and look.

"Sleeping pretty peaceful, I'd say," he said to Sierra. They laughed and Sierra kicked Cherokee, rough. But he didn't move.

Arlie knelt down, turning Cherokee on his back, and slapped his face to wake him. I knew I wasn't fixing to go anywhere. There wasn't any way I could help. Not without getting killed myself. But I couldn't leave, either.

Arlie leaned over and lay his ear to Cherokee's chest. He listened for a minute, I reckon. Then he frowned and grabbed Cherokee's wrist and felt for a pulse.

He looked up at Sierra and half whispered, "Holy Mother of God, Sierra! You've killed him!"

They stood there, not moving. Then Arlie screamed it. "You've killed your brother, Sierra!" He wasn't a person anymore. Nor Sierra. They were two wild animals, frantic and tense.

Sierra leaned down to Cherokee and checked for a pulse in his neck.

"Christ!" he screamed. "I didn't go to."

He stood and jerked his head, looking for a way out.

"C'mon!" he shouted to Arlie. "Follow me!"

He never even looked back at Cherokee. They plunged into the woods going down the mountain, ignoring the path, just got swallowed up in no time, heading away from us, running east of Houp Holler.

As soon as they were gone, I pulled out of there, running.

"Where are you going?" Mary Grady whispered as I whipped by her.

"To Cherokee," I told her.

I didn't find a pulse, either. No matter how hard I tried. His body was limp, heavy. Mary Grady had come to stand by me and I jumped up from where I had kneeled.

"Go down that path there. Don't veer off, just straight

down the mountain," I told her. "In about four or five minutes, you'll get to my house. Start screaming when you hit the yard. Get my daddy fast. Or Jonah. Or anybody, but get them fast and bring them here. Quick!"

Mary Grady just stood like she didn't understand English. I pushed my head in her direction and my eyes asked, *What?*

She read that. "Well, what if I run into them boys?" she asked. "I'm not sure it's safe —"

I grabbed this T-shirt she was wearing and reshaped it with my fist, pulling her to me. "If you happen to bump into them," I said low and even, "tell them Edie Jo Houp sent you. Tell them you're running an errand for me!" I screamed the last right in her face. Then I turned and shoved her in the direction of the path.

"Tell them," I shouted after her, "they don't like it, they can come see me. Edie Jo Houp! Got that?"

She ran, nodding and saying, "Yes. Yes. Yes. Yes." Every step she took, she hollered, "Yes."

I looked back at Cherokee lying crumpled so strange, not in a resting position, but awkward, unnatural.

Maybe cold creek water'll revive him, I think to myself and yank my T-shirt over my head as I run. Surely to God, this water would have revived Lazarus from the grave, I think as I wring out my shirt. My fingers are already numb.

I kneel over top of Cherokee and lay my cold shirt across his forehead. Then I wait and watch for his eyes to move across his closed lids. But they don't. No life moves in his body. None. At all.

Jonah was the first to come. By the time he split out of the woods on the run, I had cradled Cherokee's head in my lap and was laying my hands on his face. Touching the smoothness. Talking to him like he was still there. Just deep. Too deep to reach yet.

"Hot Shot," Jonah whispered as he came up close. "Hot Shot, what happened?"

"He's all right," I told him. Jonah. "He just can't come round. Not just yet."

But when my daddy came and leaned down to place his fingers where a heartbeat should have been, he frowned and looked at me with a look I hadn't ever seen before, nor not since.

"Edie Jo," he says in his deep rumble, "this boy you're holding. He's dead, darling."

"*No,*" I said, holding the *o* part like it was part of some song.

By that time, Mary Grady and Mama and Gramma came into the clearing.

"Baby," my daddy says to me, "you might be right. What we need to do is carry him on down to the house and try to get a medical doctor to see can he help him."

I didn't say anything. So, gentle as a daddy picking up a newborn baby, Daddy slipped his arms under Cherokee Fish. Jonah saw him struggle with the sudden weight and leaped in to help Daddy raise him. My wadded-up T-shirt fell right onto the ground, but nobody even cared.

Cherokee's arm swung loose down toward the ground as Daddy turned with him and started down the mountain. He had gone onto the path when the sound rose again inside me and I opened my mouth to let it escape. It wasn't a word, or maybe just the last part of *no,* but it came on strong and it soaked everybody standing there. Drenched them.

Jonah looked at me like I was an animal, maybe even dangerous. Mary Grady was scared and ran after Daddy. Mama's face wore a look of wonder at where the sound was coming from.

Gramma knew that sound, though. She had sung it in her own way before. She came and sat on the ground beside me and covered me with her arms so tight I finally felt steadiness on the verge of coming back.

14

Mama and Daddy didn't ask questions. I know they must have wondered, but they didn't ask why I was sitting at the sawmill with my shirt off, just my camisole keeping me from being naked to the world. Sitting there with a dead boy in my lap. I know they got some answers from Mary Grady, but even she didn't know. Not really know.

Before the sheriff drove up, Daddy put me in Gramma's bedroom with her. "Edie Jo, you don't need to come out, now," he said. "There'll be time enough later for talking to the sheriff. You stay right in here with your gramma."

And I did. I sat in her lap in the rocking chair like a giant rag doll. We listened to the voices, but all I could see in my mind was Cherokee, lying across the sofa.

I had done one thing. When Daddy had been calling the sheriff on the telephone, and everybody stirring in different directions, I had knelt down like I was praying and pulled Cherokee's mouth organ from his pocket.

I held it in my hand tight now while they took him away.

Me and Daddy, we went to the graveside service on Tuesday morning. At a place called Potter's Field. In the same cemetery with the big trees, just on the edge. I had asked Daddy could we go. I knew better than to ask Mama. I didn't ask Gramma because it would have put her on the spot with Mama. I knew Gramma understood grief, but not integration. So I told Daddy that Cherokee was a friend. That's when I knew, really knew, where Daddy stood on integration. And that's when I began to understand for myself how friendships don't shape on color.

When I asked, Daddy looked at me with kind eyes. Then he said, "Yes, Edie Jo. We'll go. You and me." I had asked Mary Grady, but she wasn't ready for that yet.

So me and Daddy picked our way around the big roots that could trip you up if you weren't careful and cause your feelings to split right out of you.

Cherokee's family was there. His sisters — not Sierra, though — and his mother and his daddy.

The service lasted about a quarter of an hour. I watched Cherokee's mother. She stood, rod still, not sobbing. Not moving. His sisters stood beside her, and I wondered where his older brother was. Probably still out west. Not even knowing there was one less member of his family beginning Sunday.

Cherokee's sisters cried. I saw. Leona, one grade behind me in school, held a purse in her hands, and the workout she put that purse through would have torn beads off it, had it been beaded. I guessed she might be going to miss him most of all. Except maybe for me. I wondered had he taught her to play the mouth organ.

The daddy in the family never moved, just stood, growing out of the big root beside his feet. I remembered what Cherokee had said about him — his "old man," he had called him: "You live at *my* house. With *my* old man." I tried hard to see Cherokee in his face, the steadiness, the way he read people and understood them. But, try as I would, what I saw was Sierra. Rat mean and cold.

The family left first and then the few other people left. We were the last to go. Saying goodbye to a pine box wasn't enough for me. When we left, I was dissatisfied, unfinished inside. It was like reading along in a book, and then having the book taken away, right at the interesting part. And never getting to finish it.

I held on to Daddy's hand as we left, careful of roots.

I could smell the cake baking when I stepped out the car door. The custard sweetness filled Houp Holler. I figured Mama was reaching out in her own way, baking a pound cake to let me know she understood I was grieving. She didn't know exactly why yet, but she saw the hurt. A pound cake might fix it, the hurt. Might help me move beyond it. Maybe so I'd be ready to answer questions about why I was up on a mountain holding a half-breed boy in my arms.

When we went inside, she came to my corner of the living room where I was slipping out of my dress behind the silk screen.

"There's a pound cake in the oven," she said.

I nodded I knew.

"I thought soon as we get through lunch, you and I might take it over to Cherokee's family."

I looked round at her from where I'd been turned away, hitching my bra.

"Your daddy has to go back to the store, but I figured you and I could take it."

"Why?" I asked when English returned to me.

Mama sat on the foot of the cot. "Because she is a mother and she lost her son." She shrugged. "Losing a child doesn't hurt less if you're Indian."

I watched her to see if she'd zing me now with the *Why were you on the mountain with a half-breed?* question. But it didn't come.

All through lunch and on the way in the car I puzzled about Mama. She sure changed tunes from time to time. One day she's screaming about Daddy trying to protect the very people who burned down Gramma's house. The next day she's taking them a cake. Of course, she didn't know for sure about the arson. It was only the sheriff's best guess. When she did find out that Sierra Fish really did it, I wondered, would she go claim what was left of the cake for spite?

"I don't know where he lives," I said when we turned down into Davis Bottoms.

"I do," she said. "I called the sheriff this morning when I decided to bake the cake, and asked him."

We turned down a street that bottomed out in a little valley. "This is the street," she said.

What a hill, I thought. I wondered if Cherokee had ever sledded down this hill come snowfall.

His house was on the right toward the bottom. If she hadn't asked the sheriff, we'd still have known because people were milling all around the yard and the door stood wide, beckoning flies from as far away as Asheville to come.

Mama parked against the curb, actually scraped it. I guessed she was nervous.

"Come on," she said, looking over at me.

I waited for her to come around and take the cake from me before I got out and shut my door. Together we walked through the yard and up on the three-step front porch. The people in the yard all turned to stare, but Mama had been stared at before. I figured Truitt's Grocery starers were more hostile than these quiet people.

When we reached the open door, Mama knocked on the frame. Leona walked over from the hall and stood looking at me.

"Is Mrs. Fish in?" Mama asked her, not even knowing she was Cherokee's sister.

Leona never looked at Mama. She just turned and went into a back room while we waited in the door. In a bit, Cherokee's mother came.

"I am Mrs. Fish," she said to Mama.

"We came," Mama said, pulling me into it with her glance, "to bring something." She held out the wax-paper bundle that was the pound cake. "Just wanted you to know we're sorry for your loss . . ."

Mrs. Fish took the cake, still warm from its morning baking. "Come in," she said. Not "Thank you," but "Come in."

It tells what Mama was made of in her core that she went on inside a house that might have recently held the very person who burned up Gramma's house. We followed Mrs. Fish into a room off to one side. This wasn't Hezekiah's house with laughter and no wallpaper. This house was wallpapered with silent people, watching people.

We sat on a sofa that had been covered with a blanket. Mrs. Fish held the cake on her lap where she sat in a lawn chair next to the sofa.

At first we sat, drowning in the silence. Then Mrs. Fish said, "He was a good boy."

It was probably the saddest sentence I would ever hear. The *was* part was bad enough, because I was still struggling with the finality of it. But I wondered did she know how good. I honestly hoped that his mama hadn't quit seeing him since he was near grown . . . really seeing him. I wondered if she ever touched him, listened to him. I was betting he never shared his dreams with her, about leaving Half Moon and all.

"I'm sure he was," Mama said.

Next there was more quiet. It was like hollering from

one mountain to the next. You had to let the echoes die before you started up again.

"Only sixteen," Mrs. Fish said next.

Mama nodded. "I know," but she hadn't.

The ragged conversation was so painful all I wanted to do was leave, but I figured if Mama was gutsy enough to come, I could at least stick with her.

I watched a fly crawl across the wax-paper bundle on Mrs. Fish's lap, joined by a second fly. I looked over at Leona, who stood with several women against the far wall. There were no more chairs. It was a small room, full of people, watching, sitting on the floor or standing.

I smiled at Leona. It wasn't much of a smile because it wasn't in me. I really wondered if there would ever again be enough joy to bring a smile. Her eyes were solemn, but the tiniest change in her mouth told me she was trying to smile back.

I looked for Cherokee's daddy, but he wasn't in that room. Maybe somewhere else in the house, but not there.

On the way home, Mama said one thing. Nothing more. "Well, Edie Jo, it was a step. One small step. But it was in the right direction."

Me? I felt it was one grain of sand on a beach. One drop of water over Niagara. What difference would it ever make in the waterfall of prejudice that flowed through Half Moon?

15

It wasn't until some weeks had gone by that the grieving set in. The days passed and I never cried a tear. I told the sheriff what had taken place, and he told Daddy they'd have to hold a deposition when they caught Sierra and Arlie and I'd have to tell what happened one more time at the deposition. Not once during our time with the sheriff, not once did I break down and cry. My feelings were so steady I could tell him just what happened and never even feel fresh sorrow. He listened so solid I could never fathom how he was feeling about me being friends with Cherokee. Didn't much care.

I thought maybe I was immune to sharp grieving like some people are to the mumps. My grieving was destined to be just a hollow feeling inside. Since I was born missing, even though not missing all my feelings, I thought I'd sung my song of grief right there on the spot when Cherokee died. I thought there wasn't any more grieving in me.

Grief doesn't come in a landslide, I found out. It seeps in while you're sleeping. First you start in dreaming. Then your wake-up time carries over the sadness. And last your whole days are filled like a tumbler of water, filled with an aching that drips over the edge and doesn't have anywhere to go to.

I had forgot what all I had thought I was missing. It wasn't enough to find that my feelings for a boy were in place. There were other feelings in place, just lying there sleeping until Cherokee was gone. My memory was a knife that cut deep inside and wouldn't leave. I knew I wouldn't ever again be able to watch someone sobbing like Mrs. Truitt had at Mr. Truitt's funeral and not feel what she was feeling. Once you go through grief yourself, you aren't the same person ever again.

The rest of July, I sat on the porch with Gramma or I moved through my life doing my chores. I didn't leave the house except for church days. I didn't look up or out. Even reading in my library books didn't interest me. I told Mama to take them on back. I just passed days, remembered Cherokee, and passed days.

Gramma's bedspread was growing right along. I watched her crocheting on the porch every day. Finally one day I asked her, "What's crocheting, Gramma?"

She stopped and looked up at me. "You loop one string all around in different patterns," she said. "It's hard to explain. I'll teach you if you like."

I shook my head. Nothing suited me these days. I didn't even bother to say thank you. "Looks like you're just making holes. That's all," I told her.

"Well, in a way," she says. "But the holes aren't what make it pretty. It's the way you work around them."

And so she taught me, and I learned. And I learned.

16

Murder is an act common to the earth, wherever you might light, but most folks won't tolerate it and won't cover for the person who did it. Sierra and Arlie didn't get far, nor hide long. They were caught and arrested at a drive-in restaurant, on the east side of Asheville three weeks after Cherokee died.

At the deposition the judge, he says to me, "Edie Jo Houp, will you tell me, in your own words, what happened the afternoon of July 12."

In my own words? I wondered who else's words I would have used. As it turned out, though, I wished about two-thirds of the way through that I could have borrowed words from somebody else. It was right after I told the judge — while I sat there in his chamber, they call it, with my daddy and him and a man taking notes — right after I told him that Sierra and Arlie had run scared. I was at the part of what happened when I tried to wake Cherokee up.

"And I wrung water from my shirt," I says. "Cold creek water. And I lay my shirt on his face and say,

'Wake up, Cherokee. It's me, Edie Jo.' And he lays there quiet as a leaf.

"'It's me,' I say louder. But he don't hear. So," I told the judge, "I lift his head to my lap and, when I get him set, I begin to sing to him. This hymn my gramma sings."

I had forgotten I did that before Jonah and them came. I hadn't remembered until that very minute. And that's when the grief chose to rise again. I had pushed that damn grief down and held it with my fist for weeks, but wouldn't you know, right there in the middle of my telling, it rose like mercury on a hot day and busted out the top of me. I did get to turn to my daddy's shoulder before it erupted all the way.

I reckon the judge understood friendship. Daddy had when I explained it to him. He and I had sat in the front-porch swing one evening and I told him from the beginning. Even about Skeeter Runyon and Cherokee nearly killing each other. Daddy understood being friends better than anybody. I never even told Mary Grady the whole of it. Just Daddy. And when I had done with it, he pulled me to him and rested his chin on my head, letting his listening pump down through me. Letting me know somebody else in the world really heard and knew about feelings that come when they shouldn't. Or at least when a whole townful of people say they shouldn't.

The judge told my daddy we were through anyway and he would leave us in his chamber until I collected myself. He patted my shoulder when he left. Then my daddy held me tight so the grief wouldn't tear my body on its way up.

I do remember wondering if the judge would really be willing to wait until I was collected again. Because I was sure it would be a while. Maybe by the time I was grown.

Collecting myself came painfully slow. Each day I was a little more whole, a little less to pieces. Cherokee never gave up trying, even when times were hard, so if he hadn't given up, neither would I.

Mary Grady and I got into a big argument over it. I knew I was on edge because of my load of grief. She should have known, too. But she pipes up and says something about me not having any better sense than to try to be friends with a half-breed. "That's what got you in this shape to begin with," she says. "You should a known better."

We were on the phone. I swear I almost hung up on her.

"What?" I asked, trying to hope she had meant something else.

"You heard me," she blurts.

There by the telephone was a list of emergency numbers to call in times of need. I looked at it now, knowing there wasn't anybody there who could help me.

Finally, I said, "I didn't go to be friends with him, Mary Grady. Not at first. But it happened. And he was a good friend. Then what you gonna do? Say, 'I can't be your friend no more 'cause your hair's black and your skin is dark?'"

She didn't answer.

"Maybe next week," I went on, "it'll be people on your side of the mountain it's not right to be friends with."

Still nothing.

"I'm not sorry for what I did," I whispered. "And if you don't want to be friends anymore because of it, then we won't."

Nothing.

So I finished up, with a stronger voice because I could hear Cherokee loud and clear, in my mind, in my memory, "I'm not sorry . . . at all."

Then I hung up the phone.

A storm blew in during the night of August 18 and knocked out power all over the county. The next day the kitchen was quiet without Mama's radio playing her country music. But it was still busy. Gramma was on the eighth day of ten-day pickles and cooking on the gas range right along.

About four in the evening, we crank up a surprise for Gramma, it being her birthday. Daddy goes into the kitchen to bring her out to the living room where we were set up. She turned the jets on the stove lower than sin and walked into our surprise.

"Law me," she gasped when she saw the balloons and

the boughten cake with candles. "What in mercy's sake have you all done!" But it wasn't really a question, because she could see what all we had done. It was just the tail end of her "Law me" part.

"I never," she finished up while we sang her "Happy Birthday."

First she opened separate packages. They were records Mama had found at secondhand stores. "You Must Have Been a Beautiful Baby" and some Bing Crosby songs.

"Well, I do declare," Gramma said. "I'll have to save my money and purchase me a record player."

Daddy just grinned across the room at me. He walks over to my cot and slides a big brown paper bag from underneath and hands it to Gramma. When she plows into it, she pulls out a portable record player.

"Law me!" she groans. "Well, knock me over with a feather!"

"That ain't all," I say. And, reaching underneath the skirt of the sofa, I slide out the last package. "Open this one."

She opened it and I thought she was probably going to faint, she drew such a breath.

"I don't know what to say," she whispered, because there in her lap sat a whole album of Irving Berlin songs. "Where did you *ever* find such?" she asked.

"Over to a rummage sale at a church near Tingles Cafeteria in Asheville," Mama told her.

Gramma fetched her handkerchief from her left belt side and blotted behind her glasses.

"I don't know what to say," she whispered. "You know, when I came to live with you all, I was mighty low. I thought I had lost everything.

"But I've come to find out, what I lost isn't nothing to what I've got."

She smiled at everybody in the room, one at a time, like it was a gift to give. Last, she looked at me.

"Edith Josephine," she said, using my full name, maybe since I was named for her, Edith, "you have had to sacrifice the most. The money I got from selling my property wasn't much, but it was enough to build a room onto this house. Your mama and daddy and I, we've been talking and we think we'll add it on where the back porch stands.

"I'll leave it to you," she said, smiling, "Would you rather have your old room back or a new room with a wall of windows?"

A wall of windows, I thought. *Where you could look out and see the trees and the sky and the stars.* Suddenly I knew. I knew my fear of the dark was on the wane and I could sit on my bed and look up at the stars and the moon.

"The add-on room," I told her. Then I got up and walked over and sat in her lap and put my arms around her neck and hugged her tight.

Suddenly, the power came back on and two lights in

the living room flooded out their corners. But power, being strong, is silent, and the only sound we heard was Mama's radio back in the kitchen, pouring out its country music.

Power is what keeps us going, though, even when we don't want to go any further. It fills us like we are electric lights and we are helpless but to shine. I found that out for myself one night in late August. I was lying across my cot one evening, listening to Jonah and Daddy sitting on the porch swing, talking about Sierra Fish and the trial coming up in November.

"A dollar parking ticket did him in," Jonah said. "He and Arlie are looking at jail till they're old men because they got careless and left a windbreaker under a bush." Jonah fell silent. "No," he said then, "that's why they got caught. Not why they're going to jail."

I suddenly cared a little more for Jonah for knowing the difference.

Daddy blew smoke out, then added, "That's right. If they're convicted and ever get out on parole, they'll be nearly through with their lives. Makes you wonder, though, why they did it . . . but only Mr. Truitt knows, and the secret died with him . . . what passed between him and Sierra. Small slights built until they broke their backs." He paused, then said, "I wish there would come about a change in Half Moon. In the world. Where people wouldn't crush each other with their prejudices.

I wish there were just one thing I could find to do to begin that."

I watched them through my window.

It was at that same window later that evening that I saw a face again. I had brushed my hair one hundred times, like always. I had laid the brush on the table by my cot and dropped to my knees to reach for my empty book under the bed when I heard a scratching on the screen. I looked up over the cot, and there, framed in the window, was a face. The light from my lamp shined on parts of that face like it was an oil painting hanging in a museum.

I froze.

Then a voice hissed, "Hot Shot! Hot Shot!"

The scream that had already begun to grow checked itself. No stranger's going to be scratching at my screen whispering, "Hot Shot."

I rose onto my knees and looked hard.

"It's Jonah, Hot Shot," the voice said, low.

"If it is," I said, "what are you scratching on my screen for at eleven o'clock of a night. Are you trying to scare me, Jonah Houp?"

"*Sh-h-h!* Keep your voice down. I got locked out. Let me in the front door," he ordered.

"Why should I?" I asked, mad now at being startled plumb out of my wits.

"Because I'm locked out," he said, irritated.

I opened the front door.

"Where you been?" I ask.

"*Sh-h-h.* You'll wake the world. None of your business where I've been."

"I let you in, didn't I?" I asked, following him to his room.

He turned at his door. "I been to Emily's and her curfew isn't till ten-thirty. I forgot my front-door key, and Mama'd have a cow this late on a weeknight."

"How'd you get home?" I whisper, going along with his story.

"My bicycle," he says. Then he just walks in the door and closes it in my face. Not "Thank you" or anything.

I walked on back past Gramma's closed door and cross the living room for my cot when suddenly it washes over me. Jonah must have been the face the other time. I stopped walking, I was thinking so hard. It was Jonah all along. His door had been shut, but he hadn't been in his room, after all. Like tonight. Nobody knew he was gone.

It didn't take a split second for anger to catch inside me. I must have exploded like a Roman candle. I reached his door in one lunge and flung it wide.

"*You* were the one!" I shouted.

He had already peeled off his shirt and he almost jumped out of his pants when I busted in on him. He made a dive for the door and shut it behind me fast but quiet.

"What the hay?" he whispered. "Haven't you got a

lick of sense? You don't go around shouting in the middle of the —"

"And you don't go around scratching on screens in the middle, neither!" I yelled.

He clamped his hand over my mouth, shoving me against the wall.

"Shut up!" he whispered, holding me tight.

I tried to bite him and he pushed even harder.

"I'll take my hand away when you promise you'll hold it down," he said, struggling to hold my arms with his free hand.

Suddenly, he stopped. A door opened in the house. We listened. I pushed his hand down and he looked at me to ask was I going to scream.

"Jonah?" Daddy's voice came from the other side of the door. "Jonah, everything okay in there, son?"

Jonah's eyes never left me. "Yessir," he said. "My radio went up loud. Sorry."

"Your mama thought she heard something," Daddy said and we could hear him walking away. Then his door closed.

My eyes never left Jonah's. I've never hated anybody so much in my life. I told him, too.

"I hate you," I whispered. And all the things I'd ever hated him for came to mind, like pictures in one of Gramma's scrapbooks that burned up. "I hate you for getting to stay in your room while I had to give mine to Gramma. I hate you for teaching me to be scared of the dark. I hate you for scratching on my screen. Both times. And for not telling us so we'd know not to be afraid. It had just been you, sneaking home. I hate you for having Emily."

I stopped to swallow back the lump in my throat, but it wouldn't budge so I just talked around it. "I hate you!" I said low and my voice cracked.

Even though tears were washing down my face, I never looked away. We just stood. Finally, he whispered, "What d'you want from me, Hot Shot?"

"'Thank you' might of been nice," I said, quiet. "But, if you have to ask, nothing."

I opened the door and got almost across the living room before I heard him. "Hey!"

I stopped but didn't turn around.

"Thank you, Edie Jo. Thank you."

I felt my name and knew he was serious. I just stood quiet to receive it. I'm not one to buck people usually, and it hadn't come easy.

Then I crossed over to behind my screen where privacy was a sometimes thing and dark a welcome cover.

17

I never let go of my daddy's words I'd heard through the window when he and Jonah had been talking. The part about him wishing he could do just one thing to start a change. What Mama and I had done was so small, with taking the cake, it was already buried under time. Only Mrs. Fish and us remembered it probably. And Leona. Maybe some of the people there.

On a hot, blistering late August Thursday, me and Mama drove down to the hardware store to get some money from Daddy so we could buy some bulbs up to the seed-and-lawn place. Hensinger's. Belonged to the son of old Mrs. Don't-You-Know Hensinger. Mama wanted to get some iris going next spring over by the creek side of the yard. Wanted to plant the bulbs as soon as cool weather hit, and Daddy had sold out of everything but tulip bulbs.

We had passed on by Pam's Soda Shop and were heading for Hensinger's when Mrs. Fish and Leona come out of McClellan's and squint at us in the glaring sunlight.

Mama stops. "Good morning, Mrs. Fish," she says.

After what all had happened with Cherokee and Sierra, I wondered if Mrs. Fish even felt friendly toward us. Her only two sons were lost, gone because of two fires, one at Gramma's. To lose a house is one thing. Losing people, something else.

She stopped. Mrs. Fish. And smiled. Smiled? I couldn't believe that came. She bobbed her head.

"Good morning," she says.

"Mighty hot day," Mama offers. What else was there? *How are you doing?* must have crossed Mama's mind, because that's what everybody in Half Moon always said on the heels of hello. It didn't seem appropriate, I guess, under the circumstances.

"Yes," Mrs. Fish answers to the hot day.

It wasn't a long exchange. Mama said she was going to set out iris bulbs and Mrs. Fish said that'd be nice. What color?

"Oh, deep purple. And white, too."

"Pretty." Mrs. Fish nods.

Then she told Mama about compost she used to start vegetables growing out behind her house. Near the chicken house, I guessed. Then, when Mrs. Fish said the compost worked well for corn, Mama told her about a new way to cook ears of corn.

"I just leave the ears in the husks and steam them over boiling water for twenty minutes," Mama says.

Mrs. Fish smiled and stuck her tongue up over a place a tooth was missing to hide a hole where the tooth had once been.

"I've always cooked corn that way," she says.

Leona, standing beside her, giggled. And that's when I had the thought. The one thing I could do. I suddenly saw the doorway Daddy had talked about — my doorway — the one chance a person might get to do something to make a difference. Me. Daddy was still looking for ways. Mama was trying. Gutsy Mama who sometimes fell down into the ditch with everybody else, going by the rules of prejudice. But Mama climbed back out and tried again, between the falling downs.

I looked at Leona and knew what I could do. It wasn't a lot, really a very small thing, but it was something that, I guessed, was going to be better than nothing. Something usually is.

That evening I asked Jonah to take me over to Mary Grady's.

"What for?" Mama looked up to ask from where she sat darning Daddy's socks.

"I've got something I need to give her."

"Well, all right. Jonah, take the car and you drive careful. You've got my two million dollars in that car." She said that last part sometimes, talking about me and Jonah.

But after we pulled onto the main road, I told Jonah, "We're not going to Mary Grady's. I need to go see Leona."

"Leona. Leona who?"

"Fish. Leona Fish."

"Oh-o-o-o no! I'm not taking you down to no Davis Bottoms, Hot Shot. If you remember, me and you like to got ourselves killed last time we drove by there together."

"Well, we ain't driving by," I told him. "We're going in. So drive."

"I'm telling you I'm not going there, Edie Jo."

I heard the switch from Hot Shot to my name. I knew either he was cracking or more resolved. This was the time to find out.

"Well then, I'll get out and walk." I said, opening my car door. We were stopped at a traffic light and I had time to hop out. But Jonah grabbed my arm.

"What're you going there for?" He held my arm tight.

"To give Leona something."

"What?"

"I'll tell you after we go. Not before."

We sat there, staring at each other. When I knew he wouldn't budge, I said, "I'll tell Mama you were the face at the back-porch screen that time." It was my ace in the hole.

That's when he let go my arm and drove on after I shut my door. We didn't even say another word, which wasn't too unusual because there never was much to say between us. Only this time, he didn't play the radio, which he did most times, scanning the dial for Elvis music.

I showed him the street. When I got out at Leona's

house, Jonah locked my door after me and turned off the lights and the motor.

I knocked on the closed door and waited. It had just started in really dark, and I had seen lights inside through a window. Even seen between the up-and-down cracks of the house boards that there were people moving inside. I studied the one little black wire that brought them their electricity, anchored by a white knob at the corner of the house. I was thinking how much power ran through one skinny wire, enough to light up a whole house, when the door opened. Leona stood there.

"Hi," I said.

"Hi."

None of that "How are you?" stuff for us. Even if she told me, I'd probably not understand how she really was. As Cherokee said that time — I was so far from where he was. Maybe I was too far from where Leona was, too.

"Could you come out a minute?" I asked. "I've got something I want to give you."

She came onto the dark porch and closed the door behind her.

I began. I hadn't practiced this. Didn't know exactly how I'd say it. "Your brother, Cherokee, was a friend."

"I heard," she said. I guessed she knew I was found holding his body.

"When he died, that night, I slipped his harmonica, his mouth organ, in my pocket and saved it to remember him by."

She said nothing.

"He used to play it up at the sawmill. And I would listen."

Nothing.

"I kept it. Meant to always so I'd never forget him. But, I got to thinking, 'Reckon Leona has anything to remember him by?'"

I would like to have said those things people say at funeral times. Things I'd heard Mama say: "He spoke of you often." "You meant so much to him." But he didn't, and I didn't know if she meant anything to him or not.

She just stood there. The one street light a couple of houses up threw some light on her face, and, from what I could see, she was steadily looking at me. Absorbing my words like a blotter, getting darker by the minute.

I'd guess we stood there, facing each other, for at least ten years. Maybe even twenty. I couldn't tell if it was a cold standoff or a warm one. I felt my underarms stinging, so I knew I was hot. But what did Leona feel?

Reaching in my shorts pocket, I pulled out the mouth organ. It was cool to the touch even though it'd been up next to me awhile. I held it out to her.

Nothing.

We just stood. I knew Jonah was watching from the car. I didn't care. Whatever she did would be okay. The feeling came that if she turned, she turned. This was my first step at reaching out, bridging the valley between us. Between our families, our lives.

Then, in a quick move, she reached out and took the mouth organ from my hand and looked at it. I wondered did it bring back a little of Cherokee to her. She didn't say. But when she looked back at me, her eyes were brim full of tears.

She never even said thank you. Not in words. What she did, though, was hold it to her mouth and run the music up and down. Then, the next thing she did was to put her arms around me and hold me tight to her. My arms were down to my sides so I couldn't hug her back, though I would have. I just stood with her hanging on to me tight. I thought she'd never let go. It was okay, though, because I knew I'd crossed over. Finally I knew where I stood. One at a time, I could accept people for who they were. Leona could come to my house. She could come drink out of my glasses and sit at my table because she was a person. A human being I had learned to value.

It had been a chance to take. When I left, I was so glad I'd taken it. Part of missing Cherokee closed up inside me like a wound on the mend.

I never told Jonah what I gave her. He never asked again.

18

Summer passed on out and school started up again. Mary Grady and I were still friends and I was glad. We were beginning the ninth grade. In four more years I would be heading out for a university, or college. But for now, the milestone on the horizon was the annual church covered-dish dinner. It was held on September 15, after preaching. I'd like to say the people in Davis Bottoms were invited, too, but they were not.

"Can I just invite Leona's family?" I had asked Daddy.

He thought about it, then said, "That family has been down enough rough roads for the time being. I don't want to subject them to anything more right yet. I'd hate to put them through what I'm afraid would go on, Edie Jo."

I knew exactly what he meant. We had surely felt the freeze after Daddy spoke his piece at the church meeting. "Not this year," he said.

I hoped that wouldn't always be the case.

Every woman in the Vine Street Baptist Church cooked up her most special dish. Gramma brought fried chicken and her ten-day pickles, and Mama — this surprised me because I was sure she'd bring prune whip — Mama took Luscious Banana Cake that had little flecks of lemon and orange peel in the white icing. She didn't have any to bring back home, either.

When we got back to the house along about four in the evening, we were all so plumb full of home cooking we were near sick. Gramma went to her room to crochet and rock off all the desserts she had treated herself to. I was sleepy, but didn't want to nap. Every time I slept, I dreamed about Cherokee. Still, I figured someday the dreams would stop, and at the same time I was scared they would. They weren't about the time when he died. They were about his music and him, the way he was. Sometimes rough, sometimes gentle. I wondered if stopping dreaming about him would mean I was forgetting him. But I knew in my heart that wasn't possible. A boy like Cherokee Fish you weren't apt to forget. Ever.

Even without Cherokee, the sawmill on the outskirts of Half Moon was still my favorite place to go. The memory of what last happened there was washed away by the memory of all the before times. So, since it was church day and it would be empty of people, that's where I aimed to go. I came through the kitchen from the back porch where my room was going to be, and Mama was climbing down from a chair after unplugging her radio.

"Where you going with your radio?" I ask her.

"To the front porch," she says. "Don't forget to eat

your prune before the day gets out from under you." She points to the covered glass dish in the middle of the table and heads on out toward the front.

The prunes were back in full force, just as tangy as ever. You could tell things were back to normal at our house with the prunes setting out again. We weren't ever going to be a family like in one of Norman Rockwell's pictures, Mama always said. Far from it. But we were a family again, and we had survived feuds and death and fire.

I waited long enough to chew the prune away from the pit, then blew the pit into the trash can on the way out.

When I passed Jonah's door, I looked in. His feet were sticking up over the foot of his bed, jogging in time to his radio music. It was Jerry Lee Lewis music, fast and hard.

At Gramma's door, I could see her sitting there in her rocking chair, crocheting on the bedspread, which had grown so it looked like she was sitting in a field of light snow. What mountain people call *a sugaring of snow*. She had her record player going, playing a song she says was her and Grandpa's favorite song. Named "Always." Irving Berlin.

From the front porch I could hear Mama laughing before I ever opened the screen door. That was something a month ago I wouldn't have bet a plug nickel would happen . . . Mama laugh. She didn't always hold to her stand on the side of integration, but she was trying, wasn't as tense, neither. And she and Daddy weren't feuding anymore. Boy howdy, Mama and Daddy weren't feuding! Far from it! They were sitting up next to each other in the swing, listening to a tune on the radio. Daddy's choice, I knew, because it wasn't country like Mama favored. It was Elvis wailing about a hotel named Heartbreak.

I took the steps two at a time off the front porch.

"Don't you stay too long, now, Edie Jo," Mama called out to me. I waved to let her know I'd heard.

I crossed over the bridge, the creek getting colder by the day, preparing itself for winter coming on. Seemed like the colder it got, the shinier the mica rocks looked lying on its bottom.

The path to the sawmill was worn down from my trips. I went up there most evenings. When I came into the clearing, I crossed on over to the sawhorse, near the mountain of sawdust.

From my belt I tugged out the empty book. I was going to have to find a new name for it. It was getting so full of poems and thoughts it wasn't empty anymore. I laid the book on the sawhorse next to me. It was a little heavier from where I had taped the arrowhead Cherokee gave me to the inside of the front cover. I rubbed it, remembering that day he'd brought it to me, made me pick hands and it hadn't been in either, had been in his pocket all along.

The creek trickling to somewhere made music of its own, telling about the mountains — the way they smell of wood fires smoking up the hollows; the way they sound with their purple echoes; the way they feel so solid and old like dinosaurs frozen for centuries, growing crusted, moss-eaten trees for scales. And, since it was the only music left, I listened and remembered.

~

From the *Half Moon Weekly* of June 12, 1961:

Miss Leona Fish, daughter of Mr. and Mrs. Elbert Fish, has graduated with honors, receiving the mathematics award for outstanding progress and excellence in achievement. Miss Fish is the recipient of a full scholarship to Mars Hill Baptist College and plans to room with Miss Edie Jo Houp, a 1960 graduate of Half Moon High School. Miss Houp, daughter of Mrs. Horace Houp, is a rising sophomore with a double major in English and Journalism.

13th Summer

You might want to know
someday
about that summer.
How it passed.
Its music,
its journey,
its shape.
But I could no more tell it than I could explain
how mica hides itself deep in rock.
That thirteenth season of warmth
locked itself deep inside,
and, like mica,
revealed its treasures
in thin layers
for all the years since.

E. J. Houp, 1995